THE CASTLE

Then she started to walk alongside the moat with its tangle of brambles, weeds and rubbish.

It looked a terrible mess, but Valeria could see that the bottom was more or less dry.

Beyond the moat, The Castle was surrounded with smooth green fields, which eventually gave way to a curve of woodland.

Deep in thought Valeria followed the moat working her way back to the drawbridge.

This was clearly not a residential part of The Castle as there were no windows in the walls and behind them were the stables and working areas.

Suddenly she was swept off her feet and dragged into the trees.

She struggled against the strong arms that held her and tried to scream.

Then she shuddered as her mouth was closed in a passionate kiss.

As her bones turned to liquid, she realised that her captor was Sir Peter Cousins!

With a long sigh he raised his lips, looked into her eyes, and sighed,

"I have waited days for this kiss."

THE BARBARA CARTLAND PINK COLLECTION

Titles in this series

THE CASTLE

BARBARA CARTLAND

Barbaracartland.com Ltd

THE BARBARA CARTLAND PINK COLLECTION

Barbara Cartland was the most prolific bestselling author in the history of the world. She was frequently in the Guinness Book of Records for writing more books in a year than any other living author. In fact her most amazing literary feat was when her publishers asked for more Barbara Cartland romances, she doubled her output from 10 books a year to over 20 books a year, when she was 77.

She went on writing continuously at this rate for 20 years and wrote her last book at the age of 97, thus completing 400 books between the ages of 77 and 97.

Her publishers finally could not keep up with this phenomenal output, so at her death she left 160 unpublished manuscripts, something again that no other author has ever achieved.

Now the exciting news is that these 160 original unpublished Barbara Cartland books are already being published and by Barbaracartland.com exclusively on the internet, as the international web is the best possible way of reaching so many Barbara Cartland readers around the world.

The 160 books are published monthly and will be numbered in sequence.

The series is called the Pink Collection as a tribute to Barbara Cartland whose favourite colour was pink and it became very much her trademark over the years.

The Barbara Cartland Pink Collection is published only on the internet. Log on to www.barbaracartland.com to find out how you can purchase the books monthly as they are published, and take out a subscription that will ensure that all subsequent editions are delivered to you by mail order to your home.

NEW

Barbaracartland.com is proud to announce the publication of ten new Audio Books for the first time as CDs. They are favourite Barbara Cartland stories read by well-known actors and actresses and each story extends to 4 or 5 CDs. The Audio Books are as follows:

The Patient Bridegroom	The Passion and the Flower
A Challenge of Hearts	Little White Doves of Love
A Train to Love	The Prince and the Pekinese
The Unbroken Dream	A King in Love
The Cruel Count	A Sign of Love

More Audio Books will be published in the future and the above titles can be purchased by logging on to the website www.barbaracartland.com or please write to the address below.

If you do not have access to a computer, you can write for information about the Barbara Cartland Pink Collection and the Barbara Cartland Audio Books to the following address:

Barbara Cartland.com Ltd., Camfield Place,
Hatfield, Hertfordshire AL9 6JE, United Kingdom.
Telephone: +44 (0)1707 642629
Fax: +44 (0)1707 663041

THE LATE DAME BARBARA CARTLAND

Barbara Cartland who sadly died in May 2000 at the age of nearly 99 was the world's most famous romantic novelist who wrote 723 books in her lifetime with worldwide sales of over 1 billion copies and her books were translated into 36 different languages.

As well as romantic novels, she wrote historical biographies, 6 autobiographies, theatrical plays, books of advice on life, love, vitamins and cookery. She also found time to be a political speaker and television and radio personality.

She wrote her first book at the age of 21 and this was called *Jigsaw*. It became an immediate bestseller and sold 100,000 copies in hardback and was translated into 6 different languages. She wrote continuously throughout her life, writing bestsellers for an astonishing 76 years. Her books have always been immensely popular in the United States, where in 1976 her current books were at numbers 1 & 2 in the B. Dalton bestsellers list, a feat never achieved before or since by any author.

Barbara Cartland became a legend in her own lifetime and will be best remembered for her wonderful romantic novels, so loved by her millions of readers throughout the world.

Her books will always be treasured for their moral message, her pure and innocent heroines, her good looking and dashing heroes and above all her belief that the power of love is more important than anything else in everyone's life.

"Over the years I have stayed in many Castles mostly in the Highlands of Scotland and on the whole they are uncomfortable, draughty and damp, but despite this there is always an atmosphere of romance that is compelling and intriguing in every Castle."

Barbara Cartland

CHAPTER ONE
1897

It was a beautiful morning.

Early mist wreathed mystery around the landscape, but behind the haze there was the promise of sunshine.

Valeria Montford exulted in the freshness of the air and the high spirits of her horse. She had cantered up a hill and now sat down for a moment drinking in the view over the Loire valley.

Valeria loved France and she particularly loved the Château where her friend, Juliette Desrivières, lived.

From where she had halted, Valeria could see, far away, the towers of the Desrivières Château.

Valeria had met Juliette at their Finishing School in Brussels. They had become best friends and at the end of the year, Juliette had invited Valeria to a house party at the Château.

"You must come," Juliette had said. "I want you to meet Jean-Pierre Delacourt."

Valeria sighed. Another young man!

Juliette was always falling in love with a different one every few weeks.

"Jean-Pierre? Who is he? You haven't mentioned him before."

The opportunities for meeting the opposite sex at the

Finishing School were not many, but somehow Juliette managed to flirt with an astonishing range of young men.

Juliette gave a little sigh.

"I met the Comte Delacourt some time ago. 'E is a near neighbour of ours on the Loire. It would be a match most acceptable. Both families wish that I accept his offer of marriage!"

Valeria looked at the set expression on her face and unusually decided not to question her friend further.

"Of course I would like to come and stay with you, Juliette, you know I always love visiting your family."

The house party was great fun.

There were a number of young people staying at the Château and expeditions and parties had been arranged.

Valeria danced and flirted with several of the young men. Laughter and gaiety were as necessary to her as food and drink. She loved being in company and enjoyed being told how attractive she was.

Last night there had been a grand ball.

Juliette's engagement to Jean-Pierre Delacourt had been announced and they had opened the dancing.

Valeria had watched as Juliette in a lovely pink silk dress circled the ballroom with her fiancé.

She had smiled and looked happily at her partner, but Valeria felt she lacked the especial sparkle that had so marked her in the adventures they had enjoyed together.

At once Valeria had been claimed for dances.

More young men wanted to partner her than there were opportunities. She had laughed and told the unlucky ones that they would have to wait for another party.

It had been extremely late before the band stopped playing and the guests drifted off to bed.

"Don't wake me up in the morning, *chérie*," Juliette had said to Valeria. "I shall be too tired for our usual ride."

And this was a shame as Valeria had been looking forward to hearing more about her feelings for the Count.

So Valeria set off on her own on a spirited stallion urging him on, feeling anxious to dismiss her worries about Juliette.

Soon they were flying down the gentle slope of the hillside, horse and rider exulting in the thrill of the ride.

A hedge came up and Valeria did not hesitate to set the stallion to jump it.

Then – disaster!

On the other side of the hedge, the ground sloped unexpectedly steeply, the horse stumbled and Valeria was catapulted onto the hard ground.

For a moment she lay there winded, wondering how many limbs she had broken.

Nervously, she tried to move first her arms and then her legs. All seemed in working order.

Wincing at the pain of her bruises, she sat up and looked around for the stallion, dreading to find that it had broken a leg.

Then she saw a horseman galloping towards her.

Almost before his horse was brought to a stop, he was dismounting.

"Are you badly hurt?" he asked as he dropped to his knees beside her. "I saw you fall. I feared you might have broken your neck."

He was obviously a fellow countryman.

Valeria was mortified.

She always prided herself on her horsemanship and her riding skill was often commented on. Now a moment's carelessness had brought down both her and her mount.

She allowed the Englishman to help her to her feet, biting her lip as she tried to think of something to say that would not betray her anger at being in such a situation.

"Thank you, sir," she managed to grind out finally. "I must see to my horse."

The stallion had by now struggled onto his feet and the Englishman gently felt down his damaged leg.

"It is not broken but badly sprained. I'm afraid you will not be able to ride him."

He straightened.

"I believe that I address Miss Montford. We met last night."

Valeria picked up the little tricorne hat which had come off in her fall and tried to remember this man from the many that had been introduced to her at the ball.

He stood stroking the neck of the injured stallion.

"Charles Waterford," he offered helpfully. "Such was the crush of eager suitors, you were unable to grant me a dance, which was a great disappointment. I am staying with some neighbours of the Desrivières and was kindly included in their invitation to last night's festivities."

Valeria could not recall meeting Charles Waterford the previous night.

She did not want to meet Charles Waterford now.

Not in such circumstances. She was not at all used to feeling anything less than perfect – perfectly turned out, perfectly beautiful, perfectly at ease.

"Such a wonderful party, wasn't it?" she remarked, wondering how she was going to extricate herself from this impossible situation. "Juliette is really such a beautiful girl and looked lovely."

"Not as lovely as you, Miss Montford."

It was the sort of response that normally she would have expected and accepted with a sweet smile. But it was said so simply and directly that Valeria, angry with herself as she was, found disconcerting.

Even more disconcerting was the reaction she felt to the way his grey eyes gazed at her.

She felt her heart give an unusual beat and the hairs on her head seemed to tingle. It was just as though she was about to lose control of who she was.

Valeria was a girl who valued her self-control. She had seen other girls dissolve into hysterics, burst into tears or blush at the admiration of men and she despised them.

She so enjoyed knowing it was she who determined how relationships proceeded – she who decided whether an admirer was to be admitted to her favour or not.

Already she felt mortified by the way this man had had to help pick her up. Now she was furious that he could have such a demoralising effect on her.

More than anything else, she wanted to remount her horse and gallop off, leaving him distraught that she would not spend time with him – and admiring her horsemanship.

Alas, this was impossible.

"I had better walk the horse back to the Château," she seethed.

Something changed in his expression, he seemed to sense her hostility.

"Miss Montford, please, allow me to switch saddles on our horses so that you can ride mine while I lead yours. The ground is rough and you cannot risk another fall."

He spoke with authority, almost as her father would have spoken.

Fuming, she looked at him more closely.

Charles Waterford was a bit older than she had first realised. He must be at least thirty. He, too, had lost his hat in his helter-skelter ride to help her and in the sun his dark hair revealed chestnut highlights.

His features, apart from his remarkable grey eyes, were indeed handsome but not memorable, yet there was a steeliness about his mouth that suggested he was not a man to be taken lightly.

He raised an ironic eyebrow at her inspection.

This made Valeria even more furious, but she knew there was no alternative to the course he suggested.

"You are too kind, sir," she said woodenly.

There was a flash of amusement in his eyes, then he began unfastening the girth of her stallion's saddle.

She watched him change over the saddles, hating every moment.

He worked quickly and efficiently. Soon her side-saddle was on his gelding and he stood beside it, holding his hands in a cup for her foot.

His calm assumption, that she had no option but to obey him, made Valeria even crosser.

But she knew that protest was useless.

So she placed her foot in his hands and allowed him to toss her up into the saddle, glad that her bruised body managed to retain its usual elegant control.

The gelding started a little, but she took firm hold of the reins and held him steady.

Charles Waterford watched her for a moment and then seemed satisfied that she could handle the animal.

"I am afraid we are some way from the Château," she said as lightly as she could manage as he started to lead her horse. "It will be a long walk for you."

She expected some flattering response, such as that no walk could be too long if he was at her side.

"Oh well, they do say that exercise is good for the soul," was all he muttered.

Which just increased Valeria's anger.

Despite herself she was rather impressed with his knowledge of the way the land lay and how quickly he led them onto a well-trodden path.

"This should lead us to the road to the Desrivières' Château," he commented amiably.

Valeria bit her lip and said nothing.

They proceeded in silence for a mile or so, Valeria keeping an eye on the stallion's gait.

Politeness dictated that she should at least attempt to engage him in light conversation to ease the tedium of their progress, but many unpleasant feelings were boiling inside her, not least of which was the knowledge that she was behaving exceedingly badly.

Eventually they joined the highway and soon after that a roadside inn came into view.

He halted the mare.

"I think we deserve a little refreshment. They may well have hot chocolate and I would appreciate an ale."

Against all her instincts, Valeria found her mouth watering at the thought of a delicious cup of hot chocolate.

She wondered if anyone would be at all worried at her late return, then she dismissed the thought. Juliette and her parents never stood on ceremony. They would assume that she was enjoying the beautiful countryside.

"Why don't we sit outside?" he suggested. "Then we can keep an eye on the horses."

He tied the two horses to the hitching post, invited Valeria to sit on a wooden bench and then went inside.

Soon he reappeared with a mug of ale.

"If I understood the French, your hot chocolate will be along shortly," he smiled. "Madame was all of a fluster at having to produce it, but I do hope she understood my fractured attempt at her language."

Valeria thought that he suddenly seemed much less sure of himself and it made her feel a little more confident.

He sat down and put his mug on the table.

"Have you known Mademoiselle Desrivières long, Miss Montford?" he asked.

She explained that they had been at school together.

Charles Waterford listened with an appearance of interest and encouraged her to talk about the school and their adventures together.

While she talked Madame brought out a mug of hot chocolate. As she thanked her in her fluent French, Valeria realised with a start that, apart from a small boy, they were now alone outside the inn. So very involved had she been in their conversation, she had not seen the other patrons of the inn disappear.

It did not seem to matter.

She tried the hot chocolate, then said with a laugh,

"I'm afraid Juliette and I were often threatened with dismissal. My father had to write me a severe letter."

"Did you have a lecture when you returned home?"

Valeria shook her head.

"Papa tries to be strict, but he loves me too much. You see, Mama died two years ago and I have no brother or sister, so we only have each other."

"How sad that sounds."

"Oh, but we have enormous fun together! He is so intelligent and loves his music. We go out to concerts and I accompany his violin on the piano."

"I wonder if I have met him," Charles Waterford murmured. "What is his full name?"

"Sir Christopher Montford, Baronet, a very ancient title," Valeria replied proudly.

She considered her father the epitome of a perfect gentleman. He was as tall as Charles Waterford and even more handsome. He knew exactly what to say to everyone and women clustered around him.

But Valeria was certain that he and her mother had enjoyed such a perfect marriage that no other female could tempt him into marrying again.

"I miss Mama very much," she sighed in a sad little voice and then laughed, "but while I have Papa I am happy. We talk about Mama often and recollect how beautiful she was and how she made our lives such fun."

He gazed at her, seeming fascinated by her words.

Then suddenly he reached down behind him.

"*No*, you don't, *you thief*," he howled.

Valeria glanced around and saw that the small boy had crept up behind her and was now securely grasped by Charles Waterford.

"He was trying to cut off your purse," he cried.

Looking down at her waist, where a small leather purse was secured by loops, she saw the boy held a knife.

She gave a small scream as she realised how nearly she had lost her purse.

"*Méchant garçon*," she shouted at him and raised her hand to give him a slap.

"No," intervened Charles Waterford in a voice that brooked no argument.

"What do you mean? He tried to rob me. We must call for the law."

"He's terrified and looks half starved."

He sounded so compelling that she swallowed her anger and took a good look at the young thief.

He could not have been more than seven years old. His eyes flickered from the man who held him to the girl he had tried to rob and back again.

Anguish was written all over his dirty pinched face. He wore a torn shirt and breeches. His bones were birdlike and small.

Valeria reached and took the knife from his hand.

Tears came to the boy's eyes and he hung his head.

"*Alors, garçon*," stammered Charles in a very poor French accent. "*Que faites vous*? Or should it be *tu*?" he asked Valeria.

"For a child, *tu*."

"Oh, darn my French. Please, you speak it so well, ask the boy why he is stealing."

Valeria was taken aback.

To her mind, if they were not going to hand the boy over to the law, he should be given a sound talking to.

But there was something about Charles Waterford and the intent way he was looking at the urchin he still held by the wrist.

The boy looked terrified and Valeria's heart melted.

Speaking gently to him she gradually persuaded the frightened urchin to give them his story.

"He says his family are starving. His father had a bad accident and lost half his leg. Now he can't work. His mother used to take in washing but she is ill. They have no food to eat.

"The boy is called Pierre and he has been trying to find work without any success. He thought stealing was all that was left to him."

Valeria looked carefully at the boy.

He now seemed less frightened and more confident. How honest were those huge blue eyes, she wondered.

"If his story is true, it is tragic," she said slowly.

Charles Waterford stared at the boy.

"You feel that maybe he is embroidering the facts?"

There was something in the way that he said it that made Valeria feel cynical and mean.

"I want to believe him, but it sounds too awful."

He stood up.

"Why then don't we go and check?" he suggested briskly. "I imagine that he lives not too far away. Ask him exactly where his home is."

A few minutes later they set out.

Pierre refused the offer of a ride on the horse.

Charles Waterford led the horses as Valeria too had refused to ride and walked holding the boy's dirty hand.

Pierre's home was further away than she thought.

The sun had burned through the morning mist and Valeria began to regret that her habit might be fashionable and well cut, but it was too heavy for today's weather.

Suddenly Pierre darted off into an overgrown track. Flies buzzed around them as they followed the small boy.

Charles Waterford suggested she stay on the road with the horses and wait there for him.

"Indeed not!" she responded indignantly. "I want to see exactly what sort of home the boy lives in."

At that moment the track ran into an open clearing where sat not so much a cottage as a hovel. Built of the humblest materials, the walls hardly held together and the roof appeared to be on the point of collapse.

Valeria went and looked inside and Pierre called to his father that they had visitors.

Immediately an old man emerged. He leaned on a crutch, one leg of his torn trousers turned up over a stump.

He looked from Valeria to Charles.

"*Monseigneur, Madame –* " he started, but his voice trailed off as though the situation was too extraordinary for him to be able to comment any further.

Pierre tugged at Valeria's coat and asked her to step inside and speak to his mother.

Valeria then wondered if this was wise and glanced across at Charles. He gave her a little nod.

Next she followed Pierre into the hovel, stooping in order not to bump her head as she entered.

It was so dark that she had to stand quite still for a moment to allow her eyes to adjust. All she could hear was the sound of heavy laboured breathing.

Then gradually she could make out a woman lying on a bed of ferns. She seemed hardly conscious.

Standing by the bed was a girl who looked a little younger than Pierre. Her dress was ragged, her long brown hair was tangled and her face dirty. But her eyes were the same intense blue and she gazed at Valeria in awe.

Pierre grabbed her by the hand and told her that he had brought a beautiful lady to meet her.

Valeria smiled.

Never had she felt less beautiful or more privileged than when she glanced around this dreadful dwelling.

Pierre seized his sister's hand.

"*Madame, voilà Rose, ma soeur.*"

In a most pleading voice she asked her brother if he had brought them any money or anything they could eat.

Pierre put his hands into his pockets and shook his head not able to meet her haunted gaze.

Tears ran down Rose's cheeks.

Valeria's heart was torn.

Regardless of the dirt floor, she knelt down beside the little girl. Removing her gloves and taking out a lace handkerchief, she tried to wipe the girl's eyes, soothing her and trying to tell her that everything would be all right.

After a while, the girl took the handkerchief, wiped away her tears and then smoothed out the damp lace on the skirt of Valeria's habit.

"*C'est très, très jolie!*" she cried in wonderment.

Valeria pressed the handkerchief into her hand.

"*Pour tu.*"

"*Pour moi? C'est vrai?*"

The girl was unable to believe that such a precious item could possibly be a gift.

Valeria scrabbled in her purse that Pierre had tried to steal from her and took out all the money it held.

It was not much, but the boy's face as she handed it over suggested that for him it was untold riches.

"*Merci, merci, merci bien,*" he cried, standing with his hands full of the coins.

For Valeria they represented the cost of a new pair of gloves, for Pierre's family, she realised, they meant food for maybe a couple of weeks.

There seemed little Valeria could do for the mother.

She rose to her feet and brushed down her skirt.

Rose stroked the fine material.

Valeria wished she could take it off and give it to the girl. Instead she took her hand and led her outside.

She looked helplessly at Charles Waterford,

"This is worse than we thought. Can anything be done?"

"I shall discuss the matter with my friends. Maybe they will know whose land this family is on, it could even be theirs. Certainly the local Priest needs to be informed."

Suddenly there came a screech from inside the trees around them.

An animal in pain reckoned Valeria.

Pierre ran off and his father gave an excited cry and Rose clapped her hands together.

They all watched until, a few minutes later, Pierre came back, his face full of smiles.

He was clutching a dead hare by the back legs. It looked as though its neck had been broken.

The father took the animal, produced a knife and proceeded to disembowel and skin it.

Valeria shuddered and, nauseated at the sight, ran back to the horses.

"It means they can have a proper meal," muttered Charles Waterford. "You cannot begrudge them that."

She shook her head, unable to meet his eyes.

Her hands trembled as she released the reins.

"Is there anything more that we can do here?" she asked, her voice shaky.

"I suppose not," he said and she knew that he must despise her.

All her feelings of humiliation flooded back and she hated Charles Waterford.

CHAPTER TWO

Juliette was very excited.

"Valeria, *chérie*, what 'as 'appened to you? You have been away so long! Where you find Lord Waterford and why not invite 'im in for drink? 'E is much the *parfait gentilhomme*. I like 'im so much."

Valeria was astonished to learn her rescuer's title.

Lord Waterford was far from her conception of an aristocrat. He might look attractive, but he lacked the dash and *élan* she associated with members of the Peerage.

He had led her stallion all the way to the Château and Valeria had not been able to keep up a conversation.

After a little she had given up.

Back at the Château's stables, Valeria expressed as prettily as she could her deep gratitude for all his help.

"I would offer you the hospitality of the house and I know the Desrivières would welcome you most sincerely, but I do not feel I should take up more of your time."

She should then have asked him to come into the Château, but she had had enough of this strange gentleman who seemed to spurn her attempts at civility.

So she had held out her hand to her saviour.

He took it, bent over it in a most flattering way, his lips almost placing a kiss on it but, in the accepted manner, not quite, then he looked up at her, his grey eyes serious.

"I am the one who should be grateful, this morning

has been an – extraordinary experience. I shall hope that, later, we may be able to meet – in a more relaxed fashion."

He spoke with a hesitancy in his voice as though he found it hard to form his phrases.

Valeria was too disturbed to notice this.

As her gaze was caught by the intensity in his eyes, she felt an odd fluttering in her heart.

Why, she thought, his eyes had silvery flecks, then she blushed unusually as though she had been caught being naughty at school.

At once she felt angry again, both at herself for her reaction – and at Charles Waterford.

He had humiliated her and had made her feel that she was lacking in grace and understanding – Valeria was not used to being made to feel she was anything less than perfect in the eyes of any of the men who flirted with her.

However, politeness was necessary.

"You will, I am sure, sir, always be welcome at the Desrivières'," she murmured and gave him her best smile.

Then she stood and watched him ride away.

As he moved out of sight, she felt a sudden chill as though dark clouds had passed over the sun.

She turned to run up the stairs to change into one of her prettiest dresses and put the whole incident behind her.

Immediately she had entered the Château, however, there was Juliette with an avalanche of questions.

Valeria could only respond with,

"He is *Lord* Waterford?"

"*Bien sur*. Did you not know? 'E want very much to meet you last night, but there were so big a crowd round *ma chère amie*."

Juliette slipped her arm through Valeria's.

"Come, we will go up to your room and you tell me everything? *Hein*? Last night you so pretty, everyone say who that lovely, lovely English miss?"

Juliette's endless chatter cheered up Valeria as they climbed up the stairs.

"It was a lovely party," she responded vaguely.

"You like Jean-Pierre? Yes?"

Valeria entered her room, took Juliette by the hand and sat them both down on the *chaise longue* at the end of the large four-poster bed.

"Juliette, my darling girl, I think Jean-Pierre is very handsome and everything a young man should be – "

Actually Valeria thought Jean-Pierre's nose was too big and his ears stuck out. Also his lips were too thick and, like Charles Waterford, he lacked a ready wit.

"But are you really so much in love with him? He seems so different from the men you usually fall for."

Juliette looked at her with interested eyes.

"*Different* – 'ow?"

"Well, he does not flirt in the usual way. He talks seriously." Valeria giggled. "He wanted to tell me about the new breed of cattle he is raising on his family's estate."

"Oh, but 'e make it so interesting, no?"

"Well, yes, I suppose so, but I have never before met any man who talks to a pretty girl like that."

"Ah, you want 'e should flirt with you? When 'e is engaged to your *chère amie*?" Juliette said provocatively.

Valeria laughed again.

"Of course not, but you know what I mean?"

Juliette grew serious.

"I do know, *chérie*." She clasped both her friend's hands. "Not all men flirt and say endless silly things. Lord

17

Waterford, 'e does not make the pretty speech, no? 'E, you would say, is serious. *Mais* 'e is very kind man and 'e 'as lots and lots of money and a great position. Papa, 'e say Lord Waterford is a man 'e like to 'ave at 'is side."

Valeria tried to suppress another giggle.

Le Comte Desrivières was a very short man and she had a sudden image of him standing beside the tall Charles Waterford.

Juliette jumped up and glared at Valeria.

"You make too much fun, *ma chérie*. I tell you, too many men flirt and – and that is all! Not many gentlemen are at all serious and responsible like Jean-Pierre or Lord Waterford."

"Juliette, darling, I am sure you are right. I do not, though, care for Charles – I mean, Lord Waterford. Come and sit down again. I want to hear everything about your engagement. When did you decide that Jean-Pierre was to be your husband?"

Juliette's fierce look did not waver.

"Ah, so, I know it! You think I do not love Jean-Pierre. That I marry 'im for money and for position. Do not deny. You think I should marry silly Henri, or the so-correct but funny Willie, or so 'andsome Freddie. *Pouf!*" She clicked her fingers. "I give *that* for Henri and Willie and Freddie."

Valeria wanted to giggle again, but Juliette looked so serious she quelled the impulse.

Julliette resumed her seat beside Valeria.

"*Chérie*, love with men like them is like rainbow! It comes suddenly, is full of colour, then after little time, it fade. With man such as Jean-Pierre, I build a marriage, a family. 'E just like Lord Waterford, 'ave great position. I know 'is family. 'E knows mine. Maybe 'is looks not so great, but 'is character, that is great. Maybe when 'e kiss me, sparks do not fly, but in 'is arms I am *confortable*."

Valeria reached out and hugged her friend.

Juliette was indeed beautiful and full of fun, yet she was practical as well. She thought deeply about her future and made her choices with her head rather than her heart.

Yet, had Valeria been someone who placed wagers, she would bet that Juliette's marriage would be a success.

"So, when Lord Waterford visit us, you laugh with 'im, smile your special smile, make 'im think you should be Lady Waterford, *hein*?"

"Oh, Juliette, do not give that possibility a second thought. Lord Waterford would never think of me that way and I don't want him to anyway. I don't like him – in fact, *I hate him*," Valeria added with passion.

"Oho, already you feel for 'im! I see it."

Juliette was gleeful.

"No, Juliette. Don't get ideas. I want nothing to do with that man. He is hateful, understand?"

Juliette gave her a mysterious smile.

"*Mais oui, chérie*, whatever you say. Come, soon we 'ave luncheon. You must change and while you do so, you tell me of your morning, eh?"

"Later. If I chat to you instead of concentrating on dressing, we shall be late and your Mama will be cross."

Valeria had to hurry, but, before she changed, she took a long look at herself in the mirror.

What had Lord Waterford seen that morning?

Last night her blonde hair had been piled on top of her head with tendrils hanging down and white camellias carefully placed above her right ear.

Today, for riding, her hair was scraped back into a

bun captured in a net that sat low on the nape of her neck. A few strands had escaped. She exclaimed with irritation and brushed the wandering tresses back into place.

Lord Waterford must have thought her some sort of hoyden!

She checked to see if her face had been splattered with mud from her fall. But the creamy skin was without blemish and her lips were sweetly pink.

Her large green eyes, though, stared back at her as she decided that her cheekbones and chin might be called classical, but she would have preferred a heart-shaped face and a cupid mouth like Juliette's.

She stamped her foot in frustration. Had she done nothing right this morning?

No wonder the noble Lord had been monosyllabic on their way back to the Château. No wonder he had found it such hard work to say something nice to her as he left.

Juliette might decide on her marriage with clinical care, but Valeria knew that when she married it had to be to someone she loved with all her heart.

Her mother and father had adored each other. Each would have given their soul for the other.

When Mama died, the light went out of Papa's life.

Valeria would demand from her marriage the same devotion her parents had brought to theirs.

*

That night Juliette and Valeria left with Jean-Pierre to a neighbouring Château for yet another ball.

Dressed in her pale green lace dress, Valeria felt at her most attractive.

She had managed to forget the humiliations of the morning and now looked forward to a delightful evening of dancing and flirting.

The Château was set by a long lake and approached across the water by a long stone bridge, edged with flaring torches.

Their carriage drew up at the bridge behind several others and across the water came the sound of violins. The night air was warm and a full moon reflected into the lake. Everything was set for a perfect evening.

The ballroom was already more than half full with guests. Running about were a number of giggling children amongst them a small girl with her arm in a sling. Valeria wondered what mischievousness had caused her accident.

Then advancing swiftly towards them she saw Lord Waterford.

At once Valeria's enjoyment of the ball vanished.

Juliette, however, was thrilled.

"My Lord Waterford," she twinkled. "Valeria 'as told me everything that 'appened yesterday morning. 'Ow you rescue 'er when 'er 'orse fall down and then that poor family! *Quelle tragedie*! *Mon père*, 'e will try to talk to neighbour who own that land. Not a good man, but, who knows! Valeria, see, 'ere is Lord Waterford!"

Valeria had no alternative but to proffer her hand,

"How very pleasant to see you again so soon, Lord Waterford."

The tall figure with the grey eyes gazed at her and again, despite everything, Valeria felt that unaccustomed tingle run again through her body.

"Miss Montford," he replied to her, bending over her hand. "A pleasure."

She sighed.

Lord Waterford did not shine as a conversationalist.

Then he turned to Juliette,

"Mademoiselle, I failed to dance with the star of the

evening yesterday, would your fiancé permit me to invite you to take the floor with me now?"

Valeria watched as Juliette put her hand in his, gave Jean-Pierre a pretty smile and then gracefully took the floor with Lord Waterford.

Once again she felt humiliation burn through her.

No use to tell herself he was only being polite – he should surely have secured her hand for the next dance before leading out Juliette.

Even worse, as she watched them circle around the floor, she noticed that Lord Waterford seemed to talk quite happily to his partner.

"*S'il vous plait*," said Jean-Pierre. "I would be very honoured if Mademoiselle Montford will dance with me."

Suppressing a sigh, although she did not find talk about cows entertaining, she put her hand in his, swept up her hem by its loop and stepped onto the dance floor.

At the end of the dance, Jean-Pierre suggested,

"I wish to introduce you to another English friend of mine. I think you will like him."

He tapped on the shoulder of a tall man with very straight polished blond hair.

"Peter, *voilà* Juliette's *chère amie*. Valeria, may I introduce Sir Peter Cousins. Peter, Miss Montford."

Valeria found herself looking into the intense blue eyes of the most attractive man she had ever met. Broad shoulders, slim hips, commanding features – he must, she decided, have Viking blood flowing in his veins.

Sir Peter took her hand in both of his, holding it as if it was a precious piece of glass.

"Jean-Pierre, I believed you had secured the most beautiful girl in the land for yourself, but now I think there is hope for the rest of us!"

He bowed deeply over Valeria's hand, his lips just skimming her flesh.

She shivered – it was as though a torch had been waved over her hand.

"Come," Sir Peter invited. "We shall dance."

As he led her to the floor, Valeria was besieged by a number of young gentlemen who begged her to save a dance for them.

Rapidly she wrote their names into her programme while Sir Peter waited, tapping his foot impatiently.

"*Enough*!" he suddenly barked. "You must all wait your turn."

Then he swept Valeria onto the floor.

It was a waltz and Sir Peter was a superb dancer. Whirling round the floor in his arms, Valeria felt she was in a dream.

"You dance like an angel," he whispered in her ear.

Valeria looked up into those blazing blue eyes and could only murmur,

"Then you must be an archangel!"

He laughed loudly, throwing back his blond head and revealing a set of perfect white teeth.

Another shiver ran through Valeria.

The ballroom blazed with candles, their soft light illuminating banks of bright flowers, their scent heady in the warm air, as Valeria, Sir Peter's hand firmly held in her back, was swept into a series of spinning turns.

She could not say anything nor did her partner seem inclined to talk as he whirled her across the floor.

Valeria caught a glimpse of Juliette dancing round with one of the Desrivières' guests.

She sent Valeria a quick, approving glance as the two couples swooped by each other.

There was no sign of Lord Waterford.

The children were still running around the edge of the floor. No adult seemed in control of them.

Breathless at the end of the dance, Valeria laughed up at Sir Peter,

"It is just as though we have put a girdle around the earth at the speed of light!"

Another flash of those white teeth.

"I feel we are still up in the clouds. Perhaps I may find you a glass of champagne?"

She longed for a cool drink, but she feared that Sir Peter would leave her side and then Lord Waterford would reappear.

"Perhaps we could take a breath of fresh air out on that loggia?" she suggested.

"I think you can read my mind," he replied, steering her towards the door into the garden.

Sir Peter somehow managed to secure two glasses of champagne on the way to the garden.

Valeria stood sipping from her glass.

The lake was edged with lanterns, their differing colours reflected in the still waters.

"It's enchanting – " she murmured.

"You are enchanting," Sir Peter came in, leaning on the balustrade and gazing into her eyes. "Why have we not met before?"

"I have been in Brussels where I met Juliette, the Count's fiancée."

"Yes, I know Mademoiselle Desrivières, a most charming girl."

From the way he spoke and a fleeting expression on his face, Valeria felt sure that Sir Peter had been one of Juliette's flirts.

"She is my closest friend," Valeria asserted.

"Of course, beauty travels with beauty."

Sir Peter grinned disarmingly at her and her heart gave a crazy leap.

"And when you are not with the beautiful Juliette, where, pray, do you live?"

"In Richmond, just outside London."

"With your parents, I suppose."

Valeria felt tears prick at the back of her eyes. She looked down at the water.

"I am afraid it is only my father and me. We lost Mama a little time ago."

"And may I know who it is who has fathered such an incredibly beautiful daughter?"

Valeria laughed.

"You are too extravagant in your compliments, Sir Peter, but I am more than happy to tell you that my father is Sir Christopher Montford."

"Sir Christopher," he muttered.

"Have you met him?"

"No, no," Sir Peter replied very quickly. "I may have heard mention of his name, that is all."

"He is known as an authority on racehorses."

"Ah, that will be it. I am a bit of a follower myself. But your champagne is finished, so I will find some more."

Before Valeria could protest, Sir Peter had whipped her glass away and disappeared back into the ballroom.

The little orchestra was now playing a vigorous and noisy number and everyone was dancing.

Valeria realised that she was alone.

Then the small group of noisy children joined her, chasing the little girl with the injured arm.

With shrieks of triumph, the children ran towards the balustrade, certain that they could now catch her.

But with an athletic wriggle, the little girl slipped through a gap in the balustrade.

She must have thought there would be room for her to stand on the other side of the supports.

Instead seconds later there was a scream followed by a huge splash.

Valeria leaned over and saw the girl's white dress spread over the water and her one hand waving frantically – then she disappeared into the water, only to re-emerge for a brief second, choking, before vanishing again.

Valeria looked frantically around.

Only the children were there, all horrified at what had happened. So noisy were the dancers, no one in the ballroom had heard the screams.

A small boy ran up and pulled at her dress to help his friend Marie.

Valeria looked over the balustrade.

She could see no sign of the little girl. There was no time to go for help if she was to be saved.

Her dear Papa had seen to it that she could swim.

"In the first place it is a most pleasant exercise," he had said. "In the second, you never know when you may need it to save either your life or the life of someone else."

Never had Valeria been more thankful either for his training or for the fact that she was wearing a dress whose bodice did up in the front.

Not bothering to undo the little buttons, she ripped it open and then pulled down her skirt and petticoat, at the same time calling out to the girl to hold on and telling the children to run for help.

Then Valeria, in pantaloons and chemise, climbed up the balustrade, held her nose and jumped into the water.

It was not cold but the depth was much greater than she expected.

Rising to the surface, she swam to the spot where she had seen the little girl fall in.

There was no sign of her.

Valeria dived down and found tough weed rose up from the bottom of the lake.

Through the gloom she could just see the white of the girl's dress caught in the clinging stalks.

Surfacing briefly to fill her lungs with air, Valeria dived again, to where the girl was struggling in the weeds.

Frantically she pulled at the strands.

Her lungs were bursting and she felt she would fail.

Then suddenly there was someone beside her with a knife, slashing with hard strokes at the murderous plants.

In seconds, the girl was free. With her in his arms, the man rose to the surface, followed by Valeria.

She broke through to the surface gasping for air to find a small boat had been hastily launched.

Eager hands pulled the little girl on board, laid her on her front and applied frantic pressure to her back.

Valeria trod water shivering and watched until the girl suddenly coughed up water.

The two men in the boat gave an exultant cry, then rowed to the bridge where the girl was carefully wrapped in a blanket and taken to warmth and safety.

Valeria sighed with thankfulness.

She looked around for the man who had managed to wield that life-saving knife, hoping to see Sir Peter.

Strong arms suddenly held her under her elbows.

"Lie back," she was told. "I will pull you to shore."

She knew that voice and it was not Sir Peter's.

For the second time that day Lord Waterford had come to her rescue!

With strong strokes he steered her back to the stone steps that led up to the Château.

There waiting for her were Juliette and Jean-Pierre, both holding huge towels.

"Wait a minute," called out Lord Waterford.

Then, in fluent French, he instructed those on the bridge to douse the torches. With a surge of excited chatter the lights were extinguished and darkness fell on the scene.

Lord Waterford then told everyone but Juliette and Jean-Pierre to go back into the Château and with more excited chatter, the bridge was cleared.

"Now, you can come up," he called out as he released his hold on Valeria.

She now reached the bottom step and then she had to stand up in her chemise and pantaloons.

Shivering as well as embarrassed, she stumbled up the steps, but Juliette was there, wrapping her in the towel.

As she was hurried up the rest of the steps, Jean-Pierre helped Lord Waterford.

"You are real 'eroine," crowed Juliette. "You 'ave saved her. And Lord Waterford, 'e is such *un gentilhome*. 'E does not look. 'E waits for you to be *respectable*."

"He speaks French! Fluently!" Valeria stammered through chattering teeth.

"*Mais oui*, why not? 'E is educated, *n'est ce pas?*"

It was too much.

Valeria burst into tears.

CHAPTER THREE

Trying to control her tears, Valeria was hurried up into one of the Château's bedrooms.

Juliette was horrified at the state of her hands.

Valeria's efforts to tear away the weeds that held little Marie meant that her skin was badly lacerated.

A doctor was found to bind up her wounds.

"Change these bandages every day and use this oil. If they do not heal quickly, come and see me, here is my card. Mademoiselle, I stand and salute your bravery."

Hot water was brought and a bowl of soup.

As Valeria sipped at the broth, finding her strength beginning to come back and listening to Juliette's chatter.

Apparently it had taken some time for the children to make anyone understand the situation.

Such was the noise of the orchestra and the dancing their story that a beautiful lady had jumped in the water to save little Marie was treated as a joke.

Then her parents heard the tale and rushed out to the loggia, to find Valeria's abandoned dress.

Someone shouted that they could see her struggling in the water to release Marie from the weeds.

The Count de Gramont produced his knife and said that only a fit and strong young man should go in.

"Sir Peter," stated Juliette, "'e say 'e should jump, but 'e cannot swim!"

"How extraordinary," murmured Valeria.

"Lord Waterford, 'e say nothing, but 'e take off 'is jacket and – and *pantalons*. 'E take the knife, 'e climb up and, *pouf*, 'e is in the water."

Meanwhile servants rushed to launch the little boat.

"We 'old our breath. When Lord Waterford rises with little Marie, we all cheer. You 'ear us?"

Valeria nodded, but she could not recall anything beyond the girl and the struggle with the weeds.

"Marie, she is all right?"

Juliette nodded emphatically.

"Marie is *petite-fille*, 'ow you say in English?"

"Granddaughter."

"Marie is granddaughter to le Comte. 'E wants to tell you many many thanks."

Juliette hugged her friend.

"All say that you are 'eroine. You 'ave such such *courage*, *chérie*. I could not jump like that, never!"

She gave a theatrical shudder.

"Of course you could, if there was nobody else. It was only me, you see. Sir Peter had gone to find us more champagne, though from what you say, he would not have been able to help even if he had been there."

"Ah, Sir Peter! 'E is so attractive, *n'est ce pas*?"

"He said that he knows you well and he appears to be great friends with your Jean-Pierre."

A twinkle appeared in Juliette's eyes.

"Once we were great friends. Once – " she let the sentence die away, a misty look on her face.

"And now you are engaged to Jean-Pierre – "

"Of course. And we shall be very very 'appy."

Then there was a knock on the door and Madame du Goncourt, Marie's mother, entered to give her profound thanks to Valeria.

"It is Lord Waterford you should thank," Valeria suggested in French. "Without him, I am afraid that your daughter could not have been rescued."

"But you gave her so much hope," said Madame du Goncourt. "She says she thought she would die, but then came an angel and told her she would live."

Valeria felt very humble.

She had not thought that she was being brave when she jumped in, only that a child was in deadly danger.

"And Lord Waterford, is he all right?" she asked in a small voice.

This man had a knack of humiliating her.

How could he pretend that his French was so bad that *she* should question the urchin boy this morning?

It could only have been that he wanted her to learn how the poor lived. Had she given him the impression she automatically assumed that they were all thieves and not worth bothering with?

"Oh, Lord Waterford is fine. His hands have been bandaged, but the doctor says they are not nearly so bad as yours – he had the knife. He is full of admiration for the way you went to the help of my darling daughter."

Was he really? Or did he just think she had been foolhardy?

She told herself she did not care what he thought.

Later Juliette told her they were to stay the night at the Château.

"Is Lord Waterford to stay as well?"

Valeria was filled with both dread that she would have to encounter him the following morning and a certain

31

strange excitement that they would be sleeping under the same roof.

Juliette shook her head. He had refused the offer of a bed.

He claimed that his part in the rescue had been no more testing than a morning swim.

No doubt, Valeria reflected numbly, he considered that too much fuss was being made of her role.

*

The next day Valeria returned to the Desrivières' Château with the profound thanks of both the little girl's parents and the de Gramonts reverberating in her ears.

She had visited Marie in bed.

The girl was pale, but otherwise seemingly full of life. Valeria laughed when the girl sweetly thanked her.

"Do be more careful in future," she advised, kissing her cheek. "You may not have Lord Waterford to rescue you next time."

"I needed you – *both*," Marie replied in a breathless voice. "You are – my guardian angels now."

"Soon this guardian angel will be back in England, so make sure you do not need her," Valeria teased her.

Back at Juliette's home, she realised her repeated diving into the water and her struggles to release Marie had taken more out of her than she had initially realised.

That afternoon all she wanted to do was relax in the drawing room and listen to Juliette playing the piano.

Her eyes half closed and listening to Chopin Etudes she allowed her mind to drift and found herself thinking of Sir Peter Cousins.

When, therefore, a servant came in to announce that an English gentleman had called and hoped to be received by Miss Montford, Valeria was sure that it was Sir Peter.

She sat up quickly and asked for him to be shown in immediately.

Juliette, stopped her playing and smiled impishly.

"Suddenly, *chérie*, you are not *so* tired!"

Valeria pouted at her and straightened her skirt.

"Lord Waterford," announced the servant.

Valeria's disappointment was intense and the light left her eyes.

Lord Waterford did not seem to notice.

"Miss Montford, please forgive me for calling like this. I am about to return to England, but I could not leave without knowing how you were and expressing my deep admiration for your actions last night."

Valeria held out her hand.

"Lord Waterford, it is I who should thank you for coming so – so efficiently to the rescue. Little Marie owes her life to you and I think I may too."

He bowed over her hand with none of Sir Peter's flourish.

"Nonsense. If you had had that knife, you would have been able to do what I did and sooner."

He turned to greet Juliette, who invited him to stay, then much to Valeria's chagrin, ordered tea to be served.

"An English custom Valeria 'as introduced 'ere," Juliette remarked with a sly smile.

He sat down and turned his attention to Valeria.

"But, please, tell me that you are fully recovered."

"Why, as you can see, I am quite myself."

He regarded her keenly and she felt herself flush. What was it about this hateful man that caused her to react so strangely to his presence?

"Your hands are bandaged. Are they injured?"

For a moment Valeria thought he would take one in his. Automatically she buried them in her dress.

"They are healing well, my Lord."

He gazed searchingly into her face then, seemingly satisfied with what he saw, sat back in his chair.

There was a small silence that was filled by Juliette saying that her friends were to visit a carriage collection on the following day.

"*C'est une collection extraordinaire*, it is great pity you cannot join us."

There was a short silence –

"I hope," Lord Waterford said carefully to Valeria, "that I may call on you in Richmond after you return."

"Why," she smiled. "I should be delighted."

"When will that be? When you return, I mean?"

Valeria sighed inwardly and longed for Sir Peter's charm and *savoir faire*.

"The Desrivières have kindly invited me to stay as long as I like, but my father is anxious to see me again."

"Sir Christopher adores 'is daughter," said Juliette, smiling. "But Valeria remains 'ere for two weeks, I think."

Valeria nodded.

"And I may visit elsewhere on the way home. It is impossible to say exactly when I will return to Richmond. It may be that Papa will join me on the Continent."

Lord Waterford looked disappointed.

Then tea arrived and Jean-Pierre came in with the Comte Desrivières. They seemed delighted to see Lord Waterford and soon took him off to the smoking room for a discussion on politics.

Juliette smiled as the door closed behind them.

"I think Lord Waterford like to remain 'ere with us, *chérie*. You 'ave made a conquest there."

"Nonsense," muttered Valeria. "He hardly spoke to me. He has no conversation."

"Lord Waterford is, I think, *timide*."

"Shy? He can't be."

For Valeria shyness belonged to very young men. Once past their twenties none of her friends were shy.

When Lord Waterford reappeared later to say his farewells, she favoured him with a most brilliant smile. He seemed charmed, but there no sign of a blush such as a shy man would suffer.

No – the man merely lacked presence.

*

The next day, viewing the impressive collection of carriages, she was able to contrast Lord Waterford's poor conversational skills with Sir Peter Cousin's ability to flirt outrageously with her.

"What a mermaid!" he piped up as he joined the party. "To think that I missed the chance of a midnight adventure with you! I am arranging for swimming lessons immediately!"

He bowed over Valeria's hand and once again it felt on fire as he held it in his.

"I am so devastated to find you still need bandages. Are your poor hands very sore?"

He spoke to her with a quiet tenderness that almost brought tears to her eyes.

Valeria hid her hands behind her back.

"They are healing rapidly, thank you. Tell me, Sir Peter," she hurried on, "are you a good driver?"

They turned to inspect the carriages on display.

Others in the party were exclaiming over the glories of a huge eighteenth century coach with ornate decorations, gold leaf paint and pale blue velvet upholstery.

Jean-Pierre persuaded Juliette to climb inside.

"See," he cried. "It is a carriage for a fairy Princess and you are the fairest of all Princesses!"

He bowed low to his fiancée as she sat in state.

"He is quite right," Valeria laughed to Sir Peter.

But he was gazing at a high phaeton in the shape of a swan.

"That is the carriage I see you in, Miss Montford. It would provide the perfect setting for your beauty."

The owner put his hand on Sir Peter's shoulder.

"You would like to drive this one? I had it out only yesterday – it is in fine condition and my team loves to pull it. Let me have the horses harnessed for you."

Valeria looked at the little seat perched high up on the extravagant wheels and her face lit up.

"It would be a real treat, sir," said Sir Peter. "You do me an honour, entrusting your horses and this splendid carriage to me."

It did not take long for a team of perfectly matched black horses to be harnessed to the phaeton – they seemed to be high spirited, snorting and shaking their heads.

"Let me help you up," offered Sir Peter to Valeria.

She placed her bandaged hand into his, her foot on the platform and swung herself up into the passenger seat.

Cheers came from below as Sir Peter joined her.

"There is a path that goes right round the estate," their host called out. "I suggest you take it. On your return you must do me the honour of joining us for refreshment."

Sir Peter set the horses off and the phaeton jerked forward.

The phaeton was beautifully sprung, Sir Peter had no trouble handling the eager horses and Valeria found the motion delightful.

Suddenly and unbidden the notion came to her that she would like Lord Waterford to see her sitting up here in this enchanting vehicle looking like a Princess.

Hastily she banished the strange idea, she did not care where Lord Waterford was or what he thought of her.

"How do you like this little foray, Miss Montford? And does it live up to your expectations?" Sir Peter asked, guiding the phaeton expertly around a corner.

"Indeed, it exceeds them, Sir Peter. I could wish this ride could go on for ever."

He glanced down at her with a wolfish smile.

"Shall we steal the phaeton and head for – where?"

She laughed.

"Why not Utopia? What could be better?"

"Except that it doesn't exist. I would prefer to take you somewhere in the real world. How about the Riviera?"

"We could not go too far without having to change horses," Valeria added provocatively, loving the fantasy of being whisked off to the South of France by this exciting man. "But would not the heat in Nice be too much at this time of the year?"

"Then why not let's go instead to Switzerland and walk hand in hand in flower-studded meadows?"

"Oh, what fun to stroll in the Alpine hills. Do you know Switzerland well?"

"Not well, but I really cannot think of a lovelier companion to take there. The lakes I hear are exquisite."

Back at the stables, as the horses were held by the groom, Sir Peter helped Valeria descend.

As she reached her foot to the ground, he grasped her at the waist and lifted her down in a broad sweeping movement.

A thrill ran through Valeria at the feel of his hands holding her so firmly.

"You are so beautiful," he whispered, looking deep into her eyes and keeping his hands on her waist.

She was so close to him she was sure he could hear the rapid beat of her heart.

She lifted her eyes to his and blushed as she saw the admiration there.

For a long moment they stood and Valeria was sure he was going to kiss her.

She knew she should move away, but something held her in his thrall. Indeed without his hands around her waist, she felt she would collapse.

Then from the garden came the sound of the rest of the party.

The moment was broken.

With a supreme effort Valeria drew back.

"Thank you so much for such a delightful ride, Sir Peter," she breathed.

He took her hand and raised it to his mouth.

"I could have had no more exquisite or entertaining passenger."

As the party finally broke up, Juliette then looked innocently up at Sir Peter.

"We shall be very 'appy to see you at the Château tomorrow, if you care to join us at dinner?"

"Alas, mademoiselle, I have to leave tomorrow. I have business in Cannes and then I return to England."

He turned to Valeria.

"Perhaps I may call upon you there?"

The sting of the disappointment she had felt at his words eased a little.

"Please do, my father would be delighted to meet you," she replied eagerly.

"Oh, it is the daughter not the father I wish to see. I must try and make some arrangement."

As the Desrivières' carriage carried her away with Juliette and Jean-Pierre, Valeria's eyes were fixed on Sir Peter and her mind replayed his intriguing last remark –

*

Two weeks later, Valeria returned to England.

As her train pulled into the station, she scanned the platform for the familiar distinguished figure of her father.

"Papa," she called. "Here I am."

He hurried over and she fell into his arms.

"Oh, Papa, I am so pleased to see you again."

"And I you, my darling girl."

"It's wonderful to be back to our lovely home."

Something twisted in his face. It was only for an instant. Almost immediately he was organising a porter to retrieve her luggage from the baggage van.

On the way home he was uncharacteristically quiet and Valeria grew a little worried.

"I hope nothing is wrong, Papa?" she asked finally, looking anxiously into his classical features.

He gave her a quick smile.

"No, darling. It's just I have missed you terribly. Now tell me about your stay with the Desrivières."

The rest of the trip was filled with her enthusiastic description of the events of her French holiday.

She did not, however, mention Lord Waterford or Sir Peter Cousins.

"Are there any letters waiting for me, Papa?" she enquired as casually as she could when they arrived.

"Letters, darling? No, I don't think so, in fact I am certain, for Mrs. Richards would have mentioned it." He looked closely at Valeria. "You are expecting a beau to be writing to you, are you?"

It was only a faint hope that Sir Peter might write to her. After all he had asked for her address. No man had ever affected her in the way Sir Peter had and Valeria was sure that he was attracted to her.

She gave a long sigh and realised how disappointed she was.

Immediately she followed her disappointment with the thought that maybe he was already on his way back to England and planning to call on her. Yes, she thought with a rising of her spirits, that was it.

Waiting for Valeria in the hall was Mrs. Richards, the Montford's housekeeper for many years.

"Welcome home Miss Valeria," said Mrs. Richards. "We have been looking forward to this day for a long time, have we not, Sir Christopher? Tea will be served in the drawing room very shortly. No doubt you would like to go upstairs and refresh yourself after your long journey?"

"Travelling is always grimy," she laughed as she started up the stairs. "I shall be glad to feel clean again."

She took a last look at her father as she went. She could not shake off the feeling that there was something that he was not telling her.

As soon as she could, Valeria returned downstairs, her jacket removed and all travel stains washed away.

It was such a lovely day that tea was served on the lawn beneath the graceful branches of a cedar of Lebanon.

Despite her worries about her Papa, Valeria gave a sigh of contentment as she looked across the closely-cut grass to the terrace that ran the full length of the house.

Built by the Montford family in mellow brick over one hundred years ago, it was known as The Red House.

Valeria poured out tea for her father and herself and hungrily attacked her favourite cucumber sandwiches.

"Let me take a good look at you," her father sighed, putting down his cup of tea.

Valeria laughed.

"You saw me off the train and on the journey here."

"But I need to see you properly."

His dark eyes surveyed her for a long moment and then he nodded approval.

"That school in Brussels has been a success. My lovely daughter has acquired polish, sophistication and an ease of manner that will make her the toast of Society."

Valeria smiled, but she had been studying her father in the same way and her concern for him increased.

Since they had last met, his face had become more lined and there were shadows under his eyes that had not been there before.

"Papa, what is wrong?" she asked him gently, "and don't tell me everything is all right with you because I will not believe it."

Sir Christopher gave a heavy sigh.

"I was never able to keep a thing from your darling Mama and I can see you take after her in more than looks."

He picked up his cup and sipped from it for a long moment. He then set it down again and drew his hand over his face as though trying to obliterate his features.

"This is hard for me, sweetheart. I have to confess to you that I have been the most foolish of men. I allowed myself to be swindled by a con artist, a man who lives by financial propositions that on the surface appear attractive.

"I invested more money than I had in the scheme he confidently assured would make me rich beyond my wilder dreams. Now I know I have lost everything. Our lovely home will have to be sold. There is even the possibility of *prison*."

Valeria stared at her father.

"Papa, don't frighten me. I can't believe what you are saying."

Another heavy sigh.

"I cannot blame you if you refuse ever to speak to me again, my darling."

Valeria moved swiftly to sit on the grass beside her father's knee. She took hold of his hand, held it to her cheek and looked up into his eyes.

"My darling Papa, how could you even think such a thing? I do not care what you have done, I shall always love you."

Tears came to his eyes.

"My precious girl! What would I do without you?"

"You will not have to. But are you sure it is quite as bad as you say? Have you spoken to anyone who knows about these affairs?"

He gently removed his hand from Valeria's grasp, found his handkerchief and blew his nose loudly.

"I have spoken to our advisers. There seems only one option – to sell everything I own, then go and live very quietly on a tiny income somewhere abroad."

"Oh Papa! It does not matter to me, but to think of you having to give up the family home and live in poverty, *I cannot bear it*."

He put away his handkerchief and reached again for Valeria's hand.

"There is just one possible alternative, I hardly dare tell you what it is."

"You must, dearest Papa. Whatever it is, if it could save you from penury, it has to be the answer."

She looked at her father.

"What is this alternative?"

He shifted slightly in his chair, picked his watch out of his waistcoat pocket and studied the face.

"An exceedingly rich man has asked me for your hand in marriage. *If you will accept, he will discharge all my debts.*"

CHAPTER FOUR

Valeria looked at her Papa in amazement.

"An offer of marriage?"

He leaned forward, excitement all over his face.

"It could be the answer to all our prayers. You will be set up in the finest style with a husband who adores you, and who is someone, incidentally, who I greatly admire – and I can remain in my home."

He looked towards the lovely house that meant so much to him.

Valeria could say nothing.

Her mind was in a whirl.

"He will join us for dinner tonight, my darling. I know he hopes for a favourable answer, he is very much in love with you and I believe you have formed an attachment to him. But, if the match is in any way distasteful to you, I shall not mind if you refuse your suitor."

He rose.

"I have to visit the stables. There are some matters that need to be discussed with Barkis."

Barkis was the Head Groom.

Horses were Sir Christopher's delight. He kept a fine stable, was known to breed successfully and was both a dashing rider and driver.

Valeria watched him walk towards the stables and remembered her drive with Sir Peter in the high phaeton.

He would have much in common with her father.

In a sudden blinding moment, she thought that this unknown suitor *had* to be Sir Peter.

A fire ran through Valeria's veins.

The more she speculated about this possibility, the more she became convinced that he was the man who had offered for her.

She knew nothing of his circumstances, but all the members of Juliette's circle seemed to be wealthy.

Sir Peter certainly looked the part, his clothes were fashionable with an air of flamboyance.

For a moment she remembered how conservatively Lord Waterford dressed. His wardrobe was well cut, but he was certainly not the height of fashion.

In addition Sir Peter understood horseflesh and he drove exceedingly well and was a dashing rider.

Lord Waterford had complete control of his mount, but he rode with none of Sir Peter's *élan*.

She recalled the way he had looked at her and the excitement that raged through her when he touched her.

Then she persuaded herself to be calm.

There was no certainty that it was indeed Sir Peter who had offered for her. After all they had only just met, even if something had seemed to spark between them.

Gradually, as she thought through all her Papa had told her, she began to understand exactly what it meant.

Unless she accepted this offer of marriage, whoever it was from, it was not only that her father would have to sell their lovely house and go away and live in penury, it meant too that she, Valeria, would not be able to afford any more pretty dresses.

She could not move in Society. She would not be able to stay with Juliette or any of the other friends she had made in Brussels. Even if they were prepared to overlook her poverty, she would not be able to accept because she would be unable to return their hospitality.

Her mouth dry, Valeria faced the extinction of life as she had known it since she was born.

Then she rallied.

She was young, perhaps starting life anew would be an adventure. She was well-educated and intelligent.

She could find employment, perhaps as a governess or a teacher or maybe as secretary to a Society hostess.

Papa, however, was not young.

He would find it difficult, nay, impossible to work. Without his horses, his ancestral home, his London Clubs and Social circle, he would be lost.

Valeria remembered the joy he found in his home. Though it had been in his family for so many years, it had been her Mama who had brought it to life.

"Some people would call this house a museum," he had once said to her, "I call it a home."

For Valeria the house was imbued with the spirit of her beloved Mama. She knew that it was the same for her father. It would break his heart if the house had to be sold.

Valeria wished that she could find the man who had brought her Papa to this pass. She would, she declared to herself, see him ruined.

If this proposal of marriage could save her father, it was her duty to accept it as the least she could do for one who loved her and made her darling mother so very happy.

Then, remembering how much in love her parents had always been with each other, Valeria wondered how she could bear to marry a man she was not in love with.

She was not like Juliette, happy to be engaged to someone she liked but did not love, confidently expecting she would find happiness with him.

That sort of marriage was not what Valeria wanted.

Then a picture of her Papa, lost without his home and friends, having to survive on nothing, filled her mind.

She rose and returned to the house.

When Papa came back from the stables, she would ask him the name of this suitor.

If indeed it turned out to be Sir Peter, there would be no problem. Her father would be saved and she would be the happiest girl in the world.

And if it was not Sir Peter?

Valeria thought of the various young gentlemen she had been introduced to over the last few years and decided that they were all at least pleasant if not very exciting.

Several of them were heirs to considerable fortunes. Maybe one had just inherited and now felt able to offer for her and to rescue her father from financial ruin.

He had always been popular with her friends.

The thought that she could stimulate such desire for her hand was exhilarating.

Yet marriage involved so much more than the odd kiss. A husband had the right to demand she share his bed.

With a man she loved, she was sure that it would be wonderful – a way of reaching to Heaven.

But without love?

The very thought made her want to scream and run away.

Valeria tried to steady herself and be resolute.

To save her beloved Papa, she would surely be able to fulfil her wifely functions? After all, she had liked all of those young gentlemen very much.

However the more she mulled over the possibilities, the more she became sure that the man who would present himself that evening was Sir Peter Cousins.

Asking to be told immediately her father returned from the stables, Valeria ran up to her bedroom, where her maid was unpacking her clothes.

"Mary, I need the prettiest dress I own to be pressed for this evening," Valeria blurted out.

The maid, a woman in her forties who had attended Valeria since before her mother died, smiled,

"Cook's in a right state about the meal this evening. She says Sir Christopher has been that pernickety about the menu. And Mrs. Richards is all of a do-da about the table settin's. Is it the Prince of Wales what's comin'?"

Valeria giggled.

That was one man she was quite certain would not be tonight's guest – though Papa was on easy terms with the Prince, Princess Alexandra was his devoted wife.

"No, Mary. Now which dress makes me look most beautiful?"

A happier hour followed choosing and discarding one dress after another until the bed in Valeria's room was covered in a rainbow of silks, satins, taffetas and laces.

"What about your white lace dress?" advised Mary. "I think there's never been a gown that suited you better."

Valeria looked at it.

Why had she not chosen to take it to Juliette's?

But Mary was right, it was most flattering and, she realised, Sir Peter would never have seen her wear it.

"Mary, you are a genius. Please press it, will you?"

The maid disappeared, smiling broadly, and Valeria went downstairs to see if Papa was back from the stables.

He was nowhere to be found and she realised that it was not going to be possible to ask him for the name of her suitor until after she had dressed.

*

Valeria gazed critically at herself in the long mirror.

The white lace dress had a closely fitted bodice that showed off her tiny waist. The neck line plunged as low as was suitable for a young girl, the fullness of the skirt softly flowed and was accentuated by a satin bow at the back.

Her Mama's pearls glowed against her skin. There were more pearls in her ears.

Her blonde hair was piled on top of her head.

"Oh, Miss Valeria, you're an absolute picture!"

"All due to you, Mary. Thank you so much. I am sorry there are so many clothes everywhere."

"Don't you worry about that, miss, you just enjoy yourself with whoever special it is what's comin' tonight. And you be sure to tell me all about it later."

Valeria closed the door of her bedroom behind her.

By the time she saw Mary again, she would either be engaged or her father would be forced to sell their home and Mary would have to be dismissed.

A shudder ran straight through her as she walked downstairs.

In the hall a footman explained that Sir Christopher was still changing. He had sent a message to say he hoped that if he were not down before their guest arrived, Valeria would do the honours.

Valeria sighed as she went into the drawing room.

As she sat and waited, she tried to remember all the good advice her Mama had given her.

"When meeting anyone, try and make yourself so fascinating they will want to meet you again," she had said.

Valeria smiled to herself.

It seemed she had made herself so fascinating to one particular man that he wanted to marry her. She tried to hold the thought to herself like a fur wrap on a cold day.

A few minutes later the doorbell rang.

Valeria stood silently by the empty grate and tried to recognise the voice that murmured a greeting as the door was opened to him.

Expectation mounted.

Soon, she hoped, Sir Peter would be standing in the doorway, smiling his dashing smile, his eyes alight.

The door opened.

Valeria prepared a welcoming smile.

"*Lord Waterford*," announced the footman.

For a moment she could only stare at the familiar figure that came in, a hesitant smile on his face.

With a sinking heart she took control of herself and came forward, held out her hand and returned his smile.

"Lord Waterford, what a surprise. How nice to see you. Are you maybe dining in the neighbourhood? I hope my father will soon be here so I can introduce you."

She hoped that he did not intend to stay too long as Sir Peter must surely be arriving at any moment.

The hesitant smile then faded and Lord Waterford cleared his throat nervously.

"Sir Christopher – that is, we have met. Has he not mentioned the fact?"

Anxiously his eyes scanned her face.

Aghast Valeria understood that *here* was her suitor.

Once again Lord Waterford had managed to put her in the wrong.

She could feel a bright red flush of humiliation rise into her face.

For a moment she could say nothing.

She hated to lose control of any situation and she hated being put in the wrong.

"Lord Waterford – I am afraid – that is – "

He recovered his poise first.

"I must apologise. I should not have assumed that your father had told you – my dear Miss Montford, would you perhaps show me his celebrated stables? I am a lover of horseflesh as well."

Valeria clutched at this opportunity to recover her badly shaken nerves.

Visiting the stables in an evening gown was, to say the least unusual, but looking at horses would give them something to talk about other than offers of marriage.

"My Lord, I would be delighted," she replied and led the way out of the drawing room.

In the hall, Valeria instructed the footman to tell Sir Christopher where they were, then she led the way through the garden door.

"I have been away for so long that I know there will be changes to my father's stables," she said, leading Lord Waterford along the terrace to the stable yard.

As they entered the long stables with stalls on both sides, she stood still for a moment and breathed in the scent of warm horses, their sweet breath filling the air.

At the far end of the stalls one whinnied a welcome.

Heedless of her lace skirt, Valeria ran down.

"It's my lovely Annie," she said over her shoulder to Lord Waterford. "I have been longing to ride her again."

She reached the mare and caressed her nose then, as the horse bent its head, scratched between her ears.

"She is charming," commented Lord Waterford.

He was standing at Valeria's side and could easily have been speaking of herself.

Valeria felt herself caught in an electric current that ran between her and the mare and Lord Waterford.

Into her mind flashed the memory of that evening in the lake – her body against his as his strong legs drove them both to the safety of the bridge.

She glanced at him – who would have thought he possessed such strong muscles under his evening clothes.

Then Valeria became unutterably confused.

What was she doing in the stables, dressed in lace, with this man who always managed to humiliate her?

"Let me show you my father's prize stallion," she suggested hastily and moved to another stall where a huge black horse threw back his head and snorted.

"Hush, Saladin," she coaxed, holding out her hand. "I'm sorry, I don't have anything for you."

The black head was lowered and the horse sniffed at her hand then blew gently on it.

Valeria rubbed at his long nose and watched Lord Waterford assess the horse's powerful body.

"What a splendid animal."

He reached out his hand and patted his neck. The horse regarded him and then bent his head towards him.

"You have been accepted!" she cried, astonished. "Saladin does not like many strangers."

"Are there any of his offspring here?"

"Why yes."

Valeria walked from stall to stall showing off her father's beautiful horses.

And she then found, to her complete surprise, that she was enjoying herself.

Lord Waterford was most interested and asked such intelligent questions, it was a pleasure to be with him.

She also realised that he had lost the diffidence he had shown on his arrival.

It was, however, exceedingly difficult for Valeria to accept that he had made an offer for her hand in marriage.

She brought out a mare he seemed interested in and walked it up and down the cobbled area between the stalls.

He leaned on one of the stall posts and watched.

It seemed to Valeria that his gaze was more on her than on the mare.

She tried to imagine exactly how she looked to him, leading the mare up and down the stables dressed in white lace with pearls glowing on her bare skin.

She felt like laughing at the strangeness of it all.

How could Lord Waterford possibly have fallen in love with her?

Even as she asked herself this burning question, he came forward and stood with his arm round the neck of the mare, gazing down at her.

Valeria found herself surprised at how very tall he was. Surely he could not have grown since they last met? Perhaps it was because he looked so serious.

"Miss Montford, your father must have told you of my offer," he muttered, gazing at her intently. "I am afraid I am not a man who finds pretty speeches too easy, but you must be aware that I fell deeply in love with you the first time we met."

Valeria stepped away, memory flooding back.

"You pretended you weren't fluent in French," she burst out angrily. "You humiliated me."

He looked surprised.

"But you speak French so beautifully. You were so much better with the boy than I would ever have been, had I tried to talk to him, he would have clammed up."

Valeria said nothing. Once again in the presence of this man she felt confused.

Lord Waterford stroked the neck of the mare again.

"Does the idea of marriage to me seem anathema to you?"

Valeria knew her Mama would have told her to find some gentle phrases to give her time to consider how she should deal with this unwanted proposal.

Completely unwanted as far as she was concerned, but a proposal nevertheless that could save her Papa.

Instead, she found herself blurting out,

"You can't have fallen in love with me! Every time we meet something happens that makes me ashamed."

Lord Waterford looked startled.

"What are you talking about? Why should you feel ashamed? You have the greatest spirit of any girl I have known."

"I fell off at that hideous hedge. I didn't believe the French boy's tale about his terrible life. I failed to release Marie from those awful weeds and – oh – so many things."

Lord Waterford removed his arm from the horse's neck and took Valeria's hand.

He looked into her distressed face, his expression very gentle.

"You ride magnificently and I saw you before your horse threw you. You dealt so well with that boy and his family. I saw you give the girl your handkerchief and the contents of your purse. And to dive into the lake to rescue little Marie was the most courageous action ever. *It is no wonder that I love you.*"

Valeria gazed at him with wide eyes.

A strange shivery feeling ran right through her.

She pulled herself together quickly.

This was Lord Waterford.

She hated him.

The shivery feeling was all part of that.

She could not possibly marry him.

Then once again she recalled her father's situation. She felt like a rat caught in a trap.

"Lord – Waterford," she stammered. "I don't know you and you don't know me."

He gripped her hands tightly.

"I do know all I need to know about you. But I see now that I was wrong – "

He dropped her hands and turned away.

Immediately Valeria felt abandoned.

He was going to withdraw his offer of marriage and then where would Papa be?

"Look," he put his hands into his pockets and gazed at his shoes.

"I should not have come to see your father without speaking to you. I should have made sure we got to know each other better. But, after I had held you in my arms in that lake, I was on fire and as soon as I came back here, I knew I had to approach Sir Christopher."

Valeria looked at him speechlessly.

Lord Waterford raised his gaze to her face.

"Can I suggest a possible way forward? I have just inherited a Castle that is only barely habitable. I have seen your beautiful home and understand that it was designed by Lady Montford, your mother.

"Sir Christopher says that you have inherited her talent and I wonder if you would come and mastermind the restoration of my Castle? If it would make you easier, it could be a business arrangement.

"In fact," he added with vigour, "I think that would be best. My widowed sister lives with me and could act as chaperone."

The mare, tired of standing still, moved restlessly and Valeria was glad to be able to take her back to its stall.

As she was securing the gate, Barkis appeared and she handed the mare to him. She introduced him to Lord Waterford and suggested they returned to the house.

"Papa will be wondering what has become of us," she remarked lightly, leading the way out of the stables.

Valeria was sure that her father had deliberately left her alone with Lord Waterford.

She just knew she could not agree to this marriage.

When she looked at him, all the humiliation she had felt at their various meetings rushed back at her.

It was no use him telling her he was madly in love with her – *she could not love him.*

There had been moments during their time in the stables when she felt that, given some time, she might just be able to be friends with him.

But to save Papa, would she be prepared to marry someone she could enjoy friendship with, if never love?

His suggestion that she mastermind the restoration of his Castle made it seem that Lord Waterford understood her need for time, and was offering her the opportunity to discover whether they could be friends.

They walked in silence for a moment, Valeria very conscious of the height and grace of the man beside her.

Then Lord Waterford enquired,

"I was most impressed with three of the horses we saw this evening. Do you think that Sir Christopher would be willing to sell them to me?"

Valeria was sure that, with his need for instant cash, her Papa would be more than willing.

"Please do ask him," she murmured.

"Indeed I will."

As they neared the house, Lord Waterford paused for a moment and then said,

"I would certainly not expect an immediate answer to my suggestion regarding the restoration of my Castle, but I hope very much you will agree to it – "

"I will let you know before the end of the evening," replied Valeria recklessly.

CHAPTER FIVE

All through dinner Sir Christopher kept their guest entertained with stories of his equine triumphs.

Lord Waterford was most interested in horseracing and expressed his desire to increase his own stable.

Valeria took little part in the conversation.

She was content to listen to Papa and ponder Lord Waterford's proposal.

The more she thought about it, the more she felt it *could* be an excellent idea. Should she, after the Castle had been put into order, decide that she could not face marriage with his Lordship, then certainly she would have acquired the foundation of a career.

Helping wealthy owners to make the most of their homes was something that Valeria knew she would enjoy.

She had helped her mother choose fabrics and wall coverings, had gone with her to dealers to find antiques and pictures. Now she was extremely confident that her taste and approach could find universal favour.

At the end of the meal she rose to leave her Papa and Lord Waterford to their port.

In the drawing room, Valeria sat herself in front of the fire. She was sure that she would soon be joined by her Papa and Lord Waterford.

To her surprise, however, the coffee grew cold and had to be replaced before the gentlemen appeared.

Papa did not seem to think they had taken too long, but Lord Waterford came over to her and muttered,

"Your father is a great conversationalist."

Valeria said nothing but thought how someone else, Sir Peter, for an instance, would have complained that her father could have enjoyed her company at any time and it was unfair for him to keep others from her.

Valeria caught a strong hint of his cologne and was suddenly aware of his manliness.

She started to pour out the coffee and as she gave Papa his cup, she took a deep breath and said,

"Has Lord Waterford mentioned the proposition he has made me – that I should help him restore his Castle?"

Lord Waterford turned to her with a hopeful smile,

"I refrained from mentioning it just in case it was a proposition you were unable to accept. Dare I to hope you have decided that you will come and help me?"

"Yes. It is an honour I am happy to accept."

'There,' she mused. 'I have made my decision.'

It might well be one that she would come to regret, but when she saw how pleased not only Lord Waterford was but also Papa, she knew it was the right one.

Not long afterwards Lord Waterford took his leave, promising to make contact with Valeria in a few days with a suggested date for her arrival at The Castle.

"I want to ensure that all will be in place for you. I need to arrange for my architect to be available and warn my sister that rooms will need to be prepared for you."

He looked around the delightful drawing room.

"I am afraid that the décor and fabric of The Castle leaves much to be desired and I hope that you will not be too unhappy staying there."

Valeria laughed.

"You forget, I have just spent a year at a Finishing School in Brussels. The décor there was of the most basic, as were the facilities. I am well prepared for any condition, however run down."

She felt reckless.

Against all the odds, a feeling of freedom filled her. If nothing else this project would be much more interesting than filling her days with Social trifles.

After Lord Waterford had departed, Papa declared,

"I am very glad you have taken the fellow up on his offer."

"Papa, just because I would be going to help Lord Waterford with restoring his Castle, it does not mean I am going to marry him."

"Of course not, my darling girl – of course not."

He looked at her for a long moment.

"But I am willing to place a considerable wager that an engagement will follow before too long!"

Valeria flushed and felt like stamping her foot.

"I am so glad no one is offering odds for you as you would lose. If you had told me it was Lord Waterford who had offered for me, I would have refused to dine with him tonight."

"Then I am glad I didn't! But, tell me, what has the poor man done that you should take against him so?"

"He puts me in the wrong every time we meet. He is insufferable," Valeria then burst out, all her antagonism flooding back.

"I am surprised that you agreed to help him with his decorations if that is the case. Lord Waterford is a first rate fellow and I couldn't like him more. Do you know he has bought three of my best horses – and at top rates too? My finances have received a life-enhancing injection. I should be able to hang on for your engagement to be announced!"

"Papa!" exclaimed Valeria in despair, her feeling of freedom quite gone.

He waved his hand as if dismissing a small fly.

"I know, I do know. And I repeat what I said this afternoon that I would never attempt to persuade you into a marriage against your wishes.

"I think, however, my darling, that you cannot do better than to accept Lord Waterford's offer."

Valeria told herself it was quite enough that she had managed to delay any decision on the subject of marriage.

Over the following days and much to her surprise, she found herself becoming quite excited at the thought of restoring Lord Waterford's Castle.

*

The day for Valeria to travel to The Castle was grey with threatened rain.

Maybe her mood was affected by the drear weather, but the nearer the train drew to her destination, the more her feelings of optimism about this project melted away.

Questions filled her mind – questions for which she had no answers.

Was The Castle really in such a poor state of repair as Lord Waterford had suggested?

If it was, what had made her think she was capable of helping to restore it?

What was his sister like?

Would she resent Valeria's presence?

And what of Lord Waterford himself?

Was he, despite his words, going to press his suit,

knowing it would be difficult for her to find refuge from him in his own home?

Had he, she suddenly wondered, only used the need of The Castle for some decoration as an excuse to lure her?

Maybe all that was required was some new curtains or a change of wall coverings and she would have almost nothing to do but fend off his advances.

By the time the train drew in at the station, Valeria was strongly tempted to catch another one back home.

Only the thought of her Papa's desperate situation made her banish that idea.

Resolved now on seeing the adventure through, she checked her appearance in her mirror.

"You look grand, Miss Valeria," intoned her maid reassuringly. Needing Mary's support, Valeria had insisted Mary travelled with her rather than in Second Class.

Valeria gave Mary a weak smile, then straightened her shoulders.

Whatever waited for her at Waterford Castle, she would not flinch from doing her best to restore it to glory.

And she would learn how to handle its Master.

Then as the train ground to a halt, Valeria could see that an imposing carriage stood outside the booking hall.

On the platform, waiting to help her down from the carriage was Lord Waterford himself.

"This is so kind of you, my Lord. I did not expect you to come to meet me yourself."

"But of course," he smiled. "How could I not?"

Calmly he gathered up Valeria's luggage.

Outside the station, she had a surprise.

He placed Mary and the luggage in the carriage and led Valeria to a smart curricle.

"I thought that you might enjoy a drive in this more than a lumbering old coach."

She allowed him to help her into the two-wheeled sporting vehicle drawn by a matched pair of grey horses.

Lord Waterford flicked the reins and they were off.

As they bowled along country lanes, Valeria's mind instantly went back to the ride she had taken with Sir Peter in the high French phaeton.

Oh, how she wished that he was here with her now! Lord Waterford might have thoroughbred horses and be an excellent whip, but he lacked the panache of Sir Peter and his delightful conversation.

"I hope you have had a pleasant journey?"

"Indeed, the train was most comfortable, my Lord."

"My sister, Lady Stratfield, is most anxious to meet you. She wanted to accompany me, but I told her she was better occupied ensuring all was ready for your arrival."

"How very kind," murmured Valeria, thinking that Sir Peter would have insisted he could not bear to share her company with anyone else.

"My sister and I hope that you will not be too bored at The Castle. Susan, that is Lady Stratfield, is anxious to arrange some sort of Social activity, but I told her to await your arrival and ascertain your wishes."

"I am sure I shall enjoy any event Lady Stratfield would like to organise."

She had a distinct suspicion that Lord Waterford's sister would prove to be a desiccated widow who enjoyed whist more than dancing.

"How long have you been living at The Castle?"

"Not very long. I inherited from a great-uncle. My father died years ago after I graduated from Cambridge.

His estate was not big enough to prevent me following my intended career as a lawyer."

"Did you never realise, my Lord, that one day you would become Lord Waterford?"

He shook his head.

"Jack, my first cousin once removed, should have inherited. He contracted cholera after a visit to India and died last year. I think it was the shock of losing him that brought on my great-uncle's fatal seizure."

"How dreadful!"

He turned and gave her a quick smile.

"It was! I had known neither well so the shock for me was not losing them, but finding I was responsible for a large estate.

"And that I was no longer Mr. Charles Robinson, a lawyer building up a career, but now Lord Waterford and expected to take my seat in the House of Lords."

Valeria laughed.

"You sound quite put out about it, most men would consider that fortune had smiled on them."

"I think you will get on well with my sister. Susan says I should enjoy everything that has come my way."

He set the horses up a steep little hill.

"At the top of this hill we shall be able to see The Castle. Prepare yourself to tell me what you think."

Valeria admired the strength of the horses as they took the hill in fine style.

At the top Lord Waterford stopped the curricle.

And there, across the valley and on top of another hill, was Waterford Castle.

Valeria had visited so-called 'Castles' that proved to be more like mansions. This one looked ready to repel an invading army!

He looked at her with a quizzical gleam in his eye.

"Well, what do you think?"

Valeria tried to be tactful.

"It is quite an edifice," she murmured.

"Oh!"

"I mean, it has great character and it dominates the surrounding countryside. It looks as though you should be flying a flag on that square tower. And that soldiers should be patrolling the battlements. Is there a drawbridge?"

"There is and we shall drive over it.

"I don't see a moat – "

"No. What was once a moat is now more of a ditch filled with brambles and weeds. Come, now you have seen the outside, we'll speed up and you can inspect the inside."

"I shall be imagining hordes of invading Vikings or French attacking those brutal walls. Did you ever visit The Castle when you were a child and play battles?"

"No, we were not close to that side of the family. I wish I had visited. It would have been a glorious place for all sorts of games. I think I'd have pretended to be Edward the Black Prince fighting the Hundred Years War!"

For the first time Valeria felt that she had a glimpse of the man inside his pleasant but remote exterior.

She could see him in her mind's eye as a small boy charging over the drawbridge. She tried to imagine him in black armour with a silver helmet. For a second she could see him mounted on a huge black charger.

A shiver ran through her.

"Are you cold, Miss Montford? I'm sorry, I should have insisted that you rode in the carriage."

"No, no, I am fine."

Once more he had caused a disturbing sensation to run through Valeria's body.

She tried to remind herself how much she disliked him, but could only wonder why, if she really had such a low opinion of Lord Waterford, was she seated beside him hastening towards his Castle?

Moments later they approached the drawbridge.

It was certainly wide enough for a sizeable coach and the curricle had no trouble rumbling across.

As they negotiated the planks, Valeria looked over at the moat that he had described as a ditch.

That, too, was wide. It was far wider than any ditch she had ever seen, but Lord Waterford was right about the weeds and brambles. She thought they would be as much of a deterrent as water for anyone wanting to cross it.

A portcullis hung above the entrance.

They drove underneath this into a vast courtyard.

Valeria gasped at the size.

"Why," she cried "you could easily house an army in here."

"At some stage in the old days, I believe they did."

Lord Waterford brought the curricle to a stop. Two grooms rushed up to take control of the horses.

"Your maid and your luggage will take a little time to arrive, I am afraid. Perhaps you would care to meet my sister and take a little light luncheon?"

"That sounds perfect, my Lord."

He led the way to an ancient door covered in heavy iron studs.

Valeria followed him and entered a vast baronial hall. Its hammer-beam roof was hung with aged flags and on the far wall were displays of spears and ancient pistols.

"I see you can defend yourself, my Lord!"

"Oh, at last you have arrived," came an irritated voice.

Valeria saw that a gallery ran along one end of the hall. Leaning over it was a fashionably dressed figure who seemed at first sight not much older than Valeria.

"Do bring Miss Montford up, Charles. I can't wait to meet her."

"Certainly, Susan."

He turned to Valeria.

"As you can see, my sister is becoming impatient."

Underneath the gallery was a carved stone screen. Behind that, in a corner, was a wide spiral staircase with shallow steps.

At the top stood Lady Stratfield.

Valeria realised that his sister was older than she had at first looked.

Curly chestnut hair tied in a loose knot surmounted a pretty oval face. Sparkling light blue eyes and a rosebud-pink mouth with pouting lips suggested a lively character.

Lady Stratfield held out her hands to Valeria.

"My dear, you are lovely! I did really believe my brother when he said that you were the most beautiful girl he had ever met, but now I see he was exactly right!

"We shall have such a lot of fun together! I cannot tell you how gloomy this dreadful Castle is. How Charles thinks it can be made liveable, I cannot imagine!"

"Yet you seem happy to stay here with me," Lord Waterford interrupted gently.

"Since I have nowhere else to go, what else could I do? You see," she said to Valeria, as she led her along a stone corridor. "When my poor John, Sir John Stratfield, I should say, had that awful accident, he left me destitute."

"But you do still have your dowry," chipped in her brother. "It brings in a reasonable income."

"Only if one is content to dress in the most dowdy way, never to travel abroad and to exist with the dullest possible routine."

She opened a door and led the way into a reception room. Two of the windows admitted plenty of light but the walls were bare stone and heavy dark furniture contributed to a cold and unfriendly atmosphere.

"My dear Miss Montford, if you can help turn this ghoulish place into a home, you will be a genius."

There was a theatrical flourish to her words.

"I have every confidence in Miss Montford," added Lord Waterford. "Now it is time for a glass of sherry.

*

Early next morning, Valeria was out riding.

Lord Waterford had provided a superb mare for her use and offered a groom to ride with her.

"I would like to accompany you, but business takes me away for a few days," he had said the previous evening after a splendid dinner in the echoing baronial hall.

Valeria was surprised. She had expected him to be in close attendance while she was staying at The Castle.

However, the whole idea of a ride without him was immensely appealing.

She could sort out some of her conflicting emotions – and plan what she could suggest for The Castle.

After dinner Valeria had asked Lord Waterford how he saw life at The Castle.

"Will you be entertaining the neighbourhood or do you contemplate a really quiet Social life?" she asked, then coloured as she realised that he was hoping she would be the Mistress of this gloomy antique ruin.

"Oh, entertainment, please!" burst out Susan. "We need to hold many parties."

Lord Waterford smiled at her and Valeria realised how very fond he was of his sister.

"I would like it to be a most pleasant place to live and perhaps to bring up a family in," he muttered quietly.

This was not a subject Valeria wished to pursue.

"Are you thinking of ever opening The Castle to the public?" she asked him. "Do you want to encourage them to visit?"

"I would like to think it would be somewhere that is spoken of with admiration," he admitted. "Does that sound very ambitious, even perhaps proud?"

"Oh, Charles, you have to realise you have a great position now and your Castle needs to reflect it. I am sure Miss Montford agrees with me?"

Valeria laughed.

"I think the position is in the man, not in his home."

Susan pouted.

"Oh, that is too clever for me!"

"Susan, Miss Montford has expressed exactly what I think," volunteered Lord Waterford.

Valeria felt warmth rush through her at his words.

They were not the idle flattery she was used to, but an acknowledgement of her intelligence.

Out riding the next morning, Valeria found herself remembering his comment. Some of the warmth she had felt when he made it remained with her.

She had refused the offer of a groom.

"I am too used to riding without attendance, as you know," she explained mischievously to Lord Waterford as they said goodnight.

He had taken his farewell of her.

"I shall have left before you rise. Susan will look

after you. My architect will wait on you tomorrow and you can explore The Castle together.

"I shall return in a couple of days, you may be sure I shall not be away a moment longer than I have to. There are matters to be sorted out about the estate. My lawyer, who was my great-uncle's, is old and of uncertain health. I decided I could not ask him to make the journey here."

What a very considerate man Lord Waterford was, Valeria thought, as she lay in bed and slipped into sleep.

*

Valeria had wakened to a morning that was bright and clear and the gloom of the previous day had vanished and she rode out eagerly.

A little way away from The Castle, she came across a large empty house. Low and rambling, it was surrounded by an overgrown garden that almost hid it from view.

There was something of *Sleeping Beauty's Palace* about the place.

Coming down the lane towards her was an elderly man wearing a smock and carrying a staff.

Valeria asked if he knew who owned the house.

"That be 'is Lordship's."

"Lord Waterford's, you mean?"

"Aye."

He tipped his hat to her.

Valeria thanked him and rode on her way, up onto open country.

'What,' she wondered, 'did Lord Waterford intend doing with this place? It could indeed be made into a very pleasant home.'

She spurred her mare into a gallop.

She could not help recalling the ride that had ended

so badly in France, when Lord Waterford had rescued her. She waited for the feeling of humiliation to wash over her again and was most surprised to find that she recalled not the humiliation but his kindness and understanding.

Suddenly there were hooves galloping behind her.

For a moment Valeria felt panic and wished she had accepted the offer of a groom to ride with her.

There was something most insistent in the speed of the following horse, she could only imagine someone was about to kidnap her.

Urging on her mount, she turned to see who was in pursuit.

Then she gave a cry of amazement.

The horseman rapidly overtaking her was *Sir Peter Cousins*.

CHAPTER SIX

Valeria brought her horse to a halt.

Sir Peter then drew up alongside her, his horse and himself breathing hard.

"You ride fast," he cried, sweeping off his hat and bowing from the saddle, his golden head shining in the sun.

Valeria's breath, too, was coming quickly.

"What an – unexpected pleasure, Sir Peter. Do you live near here?"

"No, I am staying with friends. Juliette told me you had written to her that you were going to stay at Waterford Castle. So I took up a long-standing invitation. I recalled you said once that you delighted in early morning riding so I hoped to encounter you."

Valeria felt a fizz like champagne rise inside her.

Sir Peter had sought her out!

He had followed her to The Castle!

She had not been mistaken about her attraction for him. The already bright morning became suffused with a golden warmth.

She controlled her feelings, she knew how the game was played.

"It is such a surprise to see you on English soil, Sir Peter," she murmured demurely.

"A surprise? I would have thought that you would be looking for me to appear at any moment ever since you returned. You must have recognised how powerful your effect was on me."

He sounded perfectly serious – gone was his usual, slightly ironic patter.

Valeria was thrilled.

"You are the most beautiful girl I have ever met. In the South of France all I could think about was *you*."

He gave her one of his mocking grins.

"My hostess's daughter was not pleased, I can tell you. I knew my duty and flirted outrageously with her, but my heart was not in it and I am afraid she knew it."

"I am not sure you should be speaking to me like this," Valeria countered haughtily.

"Oh, but I have to. When I returned to the Loire, it was to see you again. I was certain that you would still be there, awaiting my return."

Valeria stilled the restlessness of her mare.

"Why you should think that, I cannot conceive, but I had not seen my dear father for so long and he required my company."

"And yet here you are, away from his side!"

"I am fulfilling a commission."

"*A commission*? What sort of commission?"

"To advise on the restoration of Waterford Castle."

He laughed.

"That wreck! It will require more than your talents, Miss Montford. The old Lord sat there within its walls and let the world go hang. He was indeed famous throughout the neighbourhood for his unsociability."

"The present Lord Waterford is very different."

Valeria found herself surprised at her vehemence.

An indefinable expression crossed Sir Peter's face.

"Indeed? Intending to set this County alight with his hospitality, is he?"

For an instant she was taken aback by his sneering tone.

Then Sir Peter gave an easy laugh.

"I am sure he will prove to be an excellent landlord for his estates. I hope, though, he is not stealing your heart as well as employing your talents."

Valeria felt a flush suffuse her neck and face.

Gathering up her reins, she stroked the mare's neck.

"We must be on our way," she said primly. "Why not call at The Castle and meet Lord Waterford?"

"I may do so. Is his Lordship presently at home?"

Valeria shook her head.

"He has gone to London on estate business. He is expected to return in a couple of days' time."

Sir Peter raised a derisive eyebrow.

"Gone to London, leaving such a beautiful girl as you on her own?"

"Lord Waterford's sister, Lady Stratfield, keeps me company and I have much to occupy me. In fact, I must return at once, I have an appointment with the architect."

He grinned mockingly at her.

"An appointment with an architect! How business-like you sound, Miss Montford. And here was I thinking your only aim in life was to make men like me happy!"

Anger suddenly swelled in Valeria.

He was obviously suggesting she was only playing at restoring The Castle.

But before she could canter away, Sir Peter leaned

across the small gap between them and pulled her towards him with a strong arm.

"Just what a fascinating creature you are. The most fascinating I have ever met."

Then he brought his mouth down on hers in a most passionate kiss.

Valeria's bones turned to jelly.

She was powerless to resist. And indeed, she did not want to try.

As suddenly as he had gathered her against him, Sir Peter released her.

Valeria gasped as the pressure of his arm was taken away and the mare gave a shuddering neigh.

"How dare you, Sir Peter!" she spluttered, trying to sound completely outraged. Her blood, however, was still singing through her veins.

He gave her another of those smiles she could not help think looked a little sinister and put on his hat.

"Don't tell me you didn't enjoy that!"

Then he was gone.

Valeria rode at a fast canter towards the Castle with her thoughts in a whirl.

Out of confusion came one triumphant conclusion,

Sir Peter had sought her – the most exciting man she had ever met loved her! Maybe she would not have to reconsider Lord Waterford's proposal to save her Papa.

*

Valeria was almost late for the architect.

Afterwards she could not recall any impression of Mr. Fellowes despite page after page of her notebook being covered in her neat hand with comments he had made and ideas she had contributed.

Through their discussions her body seemed to throb with the burning memory of Sir Peter's kiss.

It was as if a fever had entered her blood. Almost she wished there was a medicine she could take that would cleanse it from her.

But then she would remember the thrilling thought that Sir Peter rather than Lord Waterford might rescue her Papa from financial ruin and marry her.

Susan joined them for lunch at her most charming.

After Mr. Fellowes had left, she remarked,

"My dear, what a terribly boring man. All he could talk about was The Castle."

"That is what he came for," laughed Valeria.

She did like Susan and her light-heartedness was a genuine tonic after the intoxication of her encounter with Sir Peter.

"Oh, you are as bad as my brother! Come, shall we play cards this afternoon? It's raining so we cannot go out. What I long for most is London! Do you find the country boring? Would you mind if I call you Valeria? You must call me Susan."

Valeria was delighted.

"I will be honoured. And, no, I don't find that the country is boring. I am sure that when Waterford Castle is more comfortable, you will enjoy living here more. Shall I explain my ideas about its restoration, Susan?"

"On no account! You must tell Charles everything when he returns and to have to repeat all the dreary details more than once would be too much."

Valeria laughed. How, she mused, could a brother and sister be so different?

So, as they settled down to cards, she asked Susan about her parents.

"My dear, they were like cat and dog. Mama told me that she had been forced into the marriage as Papa was so suitable. She had no idea, though, that Papa would turn into such a bully! He beat Charles as he was growing up when he tried to stop him shouting at Mama."

"Susan, that is awful! Your poor Mama, how could she bear it?"

Sir Peter was cast from her mind as she had a vision of Lord Waterford as a boy opposing his terrorising parent and her heart began to warm towards him.

Susan put down her cards on the table and looked at Valeria without any of her usual effervescence.

"My mother said I was to be sure to marry a man who was kind and laughed. I met John at my coming-out ball shared with a cousin. Papa was too mean to pay for one for me. Have you had a coming-out ball, Valeria?"

"Yes. I was very young, but I think Mama knew she did not have long to live and wanted to see me properly launched into Society. I had a lovely ball and Papa said he was so proud of me.

"Wasn't being presented to the Queen the funniest thing? Her Majesty is so dignified, but I do think she must have been terribly bored by it all. Tell me about meeting your husband."

"Sir John Stratfield asked me to dance and he was so amusing. He kept me in fits the whole time we were circling the floor. I knew that if I could marry him, I could forget all the unhappiness at home and live a life of fun.

"If my Papa had realised what a gambler John was, he would never have allowed our marriage. But he was a Baronet with a large estate and it all seemed very suitable.

"John loved his cards and he knew every gambling joint in London. I had no idea he had mortgaged his estate until he undertook a cross-country horse race for a large wager against a punishing rider. John must have known he would have to take every risk going. He fell trying to jump too high a hedge and broke his neck."

Tears filled her eyes.

"Dear Charles sorted out all the mess John's affairs were in and he made sure my dowry was safe, so I had an income. And he invited me to live with him. Charles is a wonderful brother and such a love."

Susan looked steadily at Valeria.

"I hope you can appreciate all his qualities. I am afraid our father sneered at him so much as a small boy, he learned never to push himself forward. He is – I think, the word is 'self-effacing'."

She gathered up all the cards.

"But I must not embarrass you. Charles would be so cross if he heard me talk like this. Come, I am sure you must play the piano beautifully."

The remainder of the afternoon was spent in music.

That evening at dinner Susan commented,

"Do you know, Valeria, that you are the first girl I have ever heard Charles say he admired?"

"I am rather surprised. Whenever we have met, I have shown myself in a very poor light."

Then she had to tell Susan the whole story.

She was amused but also impressed.

"I think you were incredibly brave," she said after Valeria tried to make light of her role in the rescue of little Marie from the lake.

"And I had no idea that dear Charles could be so enterprising. No wonder he is so taken with you."

Valeria blushed.

As Susan rattled on about the girls who had thrown their caps at her brother without him noticing them, Valeria could not but feel that, by reacting as she had to Sir Peter, she had been somewhat unfaithful to Lord Waterford –

Which was ridiculous because she had not agreed to marry Lord Waterford and she did not intend to.

She was here to help restore his Castle. She could not, however, deny that her initial dislike of his Lordship was dissolving into a feeling of friendship.

Perhaps if she had not met Sir Peter Cousins –

But indeed she *had* met Sir Peter and he raised such powerful emotions inside her that she was certain nothing could make her settle for a relationship based on no more than friendship.

Valeria fell heavily into bed that night in a state of confusion.

There were the many conflicting feelings for Lord Waterford and Sir Peter Cousins.

In addition there were the demands that restoring The Castle were about to place on her.

If she had had any idea what a big project it was, she would have hesitated to accept Lord Waterford's offer.

*

It was wet again the next day.

Driving curtains of rain covered the landscape and Valeria gave up any thought of riding.

As morning coffee was served, there was the sound of loud knocking at the heavy front door.

"A visitor! Who can that be? James, go and see at once," Susan called out to the footman. "At last, some entertainment," she added excitedly as he left the room.

James returned carrying a card on a silver salver.

"Sir Peter Cousins presents his compliments."

Valeria was thrilled.

Susan looked at the card with a shocked face.

Then through the door came the sound of shouting.

Valeria and Susan both rose and went to see what was happening.

Descending the spiral stone staircase, Valeria heard Lord Waterford's raised voice,

"*How dare you call on me!*"

"I say, old chap," came Sir Peter's voice. "No need to come the heavy. I only wanted to say 'hello'. Staying in the neighbourhood, don't you know?"

There was a pause and then the sound of a scuffle.

Valeria and Susan arrived just in time to see Lord Waterford manhandle Sir Peter out of the front door, then throw his hat and gloves after him.

Through the open door, they saw Sir Peter recover his balance and raise a warning hand.

"This will definitely not be the last you hear of me, Waterford. I will have my revenge, you – you – "

Words failed him and he strode away through the rain to his carriage, climbed up furiously and then drove at speed out of the courtyard.

"Charles," exclaimed Susan, "what have you done! And why are you back so soon?"

Lord Waterford shrugged himself out of his soaking coat and threw it on a chair.

"Thought you had the coast clear then, did you?" he snapped at her. "Thought it was safe to invite that bounder to call? *I'm surprised at you*, Susan."

Susan burst into tears and ran back up the stairs.

This was a side of Lord Waterford Valeria had not seen and it disturbed her, but she could not remain silent.

"My Lord, it was I who suggested to Sir Peter he call. I met him when I was out riding yesterday."

He swung round, startled.

"You, Miss Montford? You know Cousins?"

She flinched at his tone.

"I met Sir Peter in France. He was at the ball where Marie fell into the lake."

He bit his lip.

"I have forgotten – I avoided the man, I could not cause a scene in a foreign country where I was a guest."

He looked at her for a long moment.

"I have no right to comment on your acquaintances – or friends. I hope, however, that you number Sir Peter Cousins among the former rather than the latter. *He is a dangerous man.*"

A thrill ran through Valeria as she grew angry.

"Since Sir Peter is not present to speak for himself, can you let me know what it is you have against him?" she asserted, her back straight and her eyes challenging.

"No," he snapped, "I am not at liberty to tell you."

"I see. Well, my Lord, with the greatest respect, I have to point out that my friendships are my own business. I am here to advise you on the restoration of your Castle, not in any other capacity."

She watched his expression darken and prepared herself to be told to pack her bags.

Instead, very quietly, he just suggested,

"I would ask that you do not bring up the matter of Sir Peter's visit today with Susan."

Valeria remembered how startled Susan had been when Sir Peter's name was first announced.

She took a deep breath, gazed steadily at him – and realised she did not want to leave The Castle. Not like this.

"You are most protective of your sister," she said, tying to banish her anger.

"She is very dear to me. Now what ideas do you have to transform this ancient heap of stones? I finished my business in London as quickly as I could so that I could hurry back to hear your views."

His tone was unexpectedly grudging.

He had not, Valeria recognised, forgotten about Sir Peter Cousins's visit, nor forgiven her for inviting a man he hated to call at his home.

For a fleeting moment, she wondered what he had against Sir Peter.

Then she told herself she had to forget about him. At any rate until she had completed her mission.

Could she coax Lord Waterford into forgetting that she counted Sir Peter as a friend?

"I would be delighted if we could walk through The Castle together so that I can tell you my ideas," she said. "Would you mind if I went and collected my notebook?"

"A notebook? My dear Miss Montford, you have obviously put a great deal of thought into this project."

For a moment she felt he was being patronising.

Then Lord Waterford continued,

"You fetch your notebook and I will change out of my travelling clothes. I want to hear all your ideas."

He seemed to have recovered from his anger.

Maybe, thought Valeria, he would forget all about Sir Peter. She was rather surprised to discover how much she hoped he would – and also that the hope had nothing to do with her career.

It was not long before they met again in the hall.

"I have to tell you, Miss Montford, that I met my architect in London and he was much impressed with your grasp of the situation here."

"Was he?" Valeria was delighted. "I admired how professional he was in assessing the structural problems."

"Shall we sit," Lord Waterford waved a hand at the long dining table in the middle of the hall.

Seated opposite Lord Waterford, Valeria began,

"My Lord, when I asked you how you saw life at the Castle, you told me you desired a family home."

She blushed slightly as she said this and saw him run a finger round his stiff collar.

"But it was also clear you needed somewhere you could entertain as befits your station. You did not rule out, either, opening up The Castle to the public to enable them to appreciate your ancestral heritage."

Lord Waterford nodded slowly.

"You have grasped the essentials very well."

His appreciative tone warmed Valeria.

She felt she was being treated as someone whose opinion mattered. Never before had any man, not even her beloved father, behaved as if she had views worth listening to. It was a heady experience.

"The Castle is a most marvellous structure."

"In need of a great deal of restoration."

"If I understood your architect, there is nothing that need involve major work nor take too long."

"So I understand, which is a great relief. But, Miss Montford, how would you make this cold and stern interior a pleasant place in which to live?"

"The central heating your architect recommends would achieve a reasonable heat without everyone having to huddle around blazing fires. However, fires offer more than just heat, they are a lively focus of any room."

"Go on, Miss Montford," urged Lord Waterford, as she paused for a moment. His eyes gazed steadily at hers.

The intensity in his eyes raised an unaccustomed fluttering sensation in Valeria's breast.

She took a deep breath, looked down at her notes for a moment, then continued,

"I think what is needed inside is an abundant use of fabric offering differing colours to introduce warmth. For instance in this hall. Tapestries would immediately create a sense of warmth and bring the place to life.

"Tapestries! Wonderful idea!"

"While this hall would be splendid for large parties, there is a salon nearer to the kitchen which would be more suitable for dining with smaller numbers."

"I think I know the one you mean."

"In the reception salons, I suggest wood panelling and that the walls are hung with colourful paintings that are full of grace and beauty."

"Not portraits of dour ancestors, you mean?"

Valeria nodded.

"Light carpets and bright Turkish rugs should cover the stone floors. Furniture should be deeply comfortable and upholstered in rich fabrics in cheerful shades.

"Then I suggest lots of large cushions, maybe some covered in fur and displays of attractive porcelain."

"Such as you have in your own home?"

"They bring colour and lightness and a strong sense of beauty, do you not think?

"Now for the bedrooms. I think that they should all have their walls plastered and painted in pretty and warm colours that co-ordinate with the fabrics of the curtains and bed coverings."

He laughed, rose and started to pace the stone floor.

"My dear Miss Montford, you have given me much to think about. And you have managed to create for me a completely different vision of this ruin I live in."

He glanced up at the hammer-beamed roof.

"I am glad, though, that you have not suggested I install a ceiling in here, which I have to say was my sister's earlier thought."

"A ceiling!" Valeria was horrified. "No, indeed. My suggestion is that The Castle should retain as many as possible of the original features that give it its character. It would be splendid, for example, if you might consider a tourney at The Castle with everyone in medieval dress."

"Jousting, archery and all that?" he sounded caught by the idea. "Miss Montford, I knew that I could rely on you for an original vision and you have not let me down."

Valeria glowed with satisfaction.

Then she realised that he was not meeting her gaze.

His words were complimentary but his manner had changed. Instead of the warmth she had become used to, it was as if a door had closed in his mind, shutting her out.

It must be because of Sir Peter Cousins.

She felt as if she had stepped under a cold shower.

Then she tried to feel angry again.

After all Lord Waterford had no right to object to her friendship with Sir Peter.

"Charles, are you really going to spend the whole day discussing dreary building details with Valeria?" asked Susan entering the hall.

She looked sulky.

"I really hate it at your stupid Castle. Everything is so depressing, there is no Society and nothing to do. Why *can't* we go to London?"

Lord Waterford drew his sister to him with an arm around her shoulders.

"We shall. I have asked for Waterford House, our London residence to be opened and ready for us in a couple of weeks or so. You should send out invitations for a ball."

Susan looked stunned.

"A ball, Charles?"

"Have you not realised it is the Queen's Diamond Jubilee this summer? All London will be celebrating and so shall we."

The news should have been thrilling. There would be balls and receptions and delightful entertainments.

Valeria thought of the fun of whirling around the dance floor with a succession of handsome partners.

But was she going to be in the Waterford party?

"Miss Montford," he said, his expression calm and studiously neutral. "I hope you will join us? Maybe you can find the time to find suppliers for the fabrics and other items needed for The Castle?"

Afterwards Valeria would wonder what made her smile and accept the invitation with pleasure.

After all Lord Waterford had made it seem as if the only reason he wanted her in London was so that she could continue her job of designing The Castle décor.

She could not sort out her feelings.

Part of her was excited at the thought of being able to join in the festivities.

Part of her, however, immediately thought that in London she might meet Sir Peter Cousins again.

CHAPTER SEVEN

The time until the departure of the Waterford party for London sped by.

Valeria and Lord Waterford discussed in detail her ideas for The Castle and architectural plans were approved and work was set in progress.

Lord Waterford was obsequiously polite to Valeria.

He even accompanied her on her morning rides. It was as if he wanted to ensure that Sir Peter did not make contact with her.

Gradually she found herself enjoying his company.

There were times when he seemed to retreat within himself, as if he remembered her friendship with Sir Peter and could not forgive it.

On one morning ride, they passed the house she had noticed on her first outing from The Castle.

"What plans have you for this place, my Lord?" she asked, pointing at the house, half hidden behind its hedge.

He paused, as though trying to think of a suitable answer and then replied in a throwaway tone,

"Nothing in particular. Without doubt I will find it useful for something."

Valeria was immediately sure that he was trying to conceal his real intentions.

He obviously knew what he was going to do with the house. Why was he so secretive? Why could he not be as open with her as he had been when she first came here?

"I thought at one time that Susan might like to live here," he added after a moment. "But she says it's far too big and too expensive to maintain. In any event she prefers life in London. As you are learning, she needs company."

"I like Susan very much," she commented, turning away from the hidden house. "It must have been a terrible shock for her to be widowed at such a young age."

Lord Waterford nodded.

"She is still finding it rather difficult to rebuild her life and that is why I am so concerned about her."

He dug his heels into his mount and cantered on, leaving Valeria to follow.

Later on that day, he looked up from an architect's drawing straight at Valeria.

"Miss Montford, are you quite happy to accompany us to London for the Jubilee celebrations? You would not prefer to be at your home with your father? I do not want you to feel under any pressure. I recall how it was settled you should come to The Castle. This trip to London was no part of the arrangement."

Valeria was startled and immediately felt uneasy.

Had he regretted asking her to accompany him and Susan to London? Was he tiring of her company?

She swallowed hard.

"I thought that staying in London would mean that I could source fabrics and accessories for The Castle."

"Of course," Lord Waterford agreed instantly.

"I would, though, like to spend a few days at home with Papa before going to London. Apart from anything else, I need to arrange for a suitable wardrobe. It seems as if the whole of London Society mean to hold *soirées*, balls, dinners, luncheons and whatever else. I may have to bring more than one trunk with me."

"As many as you like, but you needn't worry about your wardrobe, as you are always so beautifully dressed."

She was pleased and stunned at his compliment.

From any other man, she would have accepted it as no more than her due.

From him so unflirtatious and sparing in personal remarks, it seemed valuable.

*

The next afternoon, Lord Waterford was busy with his factor on estate business and Valeria decided to check out an idea she had for the exterior of The Castle.

She put on stout shoes and wrapped a shawl around her shoulders to protect herself from the stiff breeze.

A steep slope led down from the wide courtyard to the entrance portico with its portcullis and heavy wooden door. She walked out over the drawbridge.

Then she started to walk alongside the moat with its tangle of brambles, weeds and rubbish.

It looked a terrible mess, but Valeria could see that the bottom was more or less dry.

Beyond the moat, The Castle was surrounded with smooth green fields, which eventually gave way to a curve of woodland.

Deep in thought Valeria followed the moat working her way back to the drawbridge.

This was clearly not a residential part of The Castle as there were no windows in the walls and behind them were the stables and working areas.

Suddenly she was swept off her feet and dragged into the trees.

She struggled against the strong arms that held her and tried to scream.

Then she shuddered as her mouth was closed in a passionate kiss.

As her bones turned to liquid, she realised that her captor was Sir Peter Cousins!

With a long sigh he raised his lips, looked into her eyes, and breathed,

"I have waited days for this kiss. I have haunted this bloody Castle, watching you and that damned Peer ride out together, laughing as you went. I tell you, for ten pins I would have pulled him from his horse and beaten him into the ground.

"And then, this afternoon, there you were, walking all alone straight into my arms. How could you keep me waiting so long?"

Her blood racing through her veins, Valeria tried to control her speech.

"How dare you grab me like that," she screamed.

"Oh, don't try outrage, my girl, you know you have been longing for me just as much as I have been for you!"

She gazed at his blazing blue eyes, his handsome face, the bare blond hair and knew she could no more deny the way he aroused her than deny that the sun rose in the sky every morning.

"Tell me why Lord Waterford threw you out of The Castle," she demanded.

A curious expression came over his face.

"You mean that you have heard nothing from either him or Susan?"

So Sir Peter had been familiar enough with Lady Stratfield to call her by her Christian name!

She gazed belligerently back at him.

"I guessed it must have been something serious."

He released her, his hand only lightly resting on her shoulder as he leant back against a tree trunk.

"It was a case of misunderstandings and a tragedy."

He glanced at The Castle.

"I was a friend of John Stratfield, Susan's husband – a close friend."

He looked Valeria full in the face again.

"Sadly the Waterfords held me responsible for the race in which he lost his life."

He dropped his hand and gave an elegant shrug.

"Nothing I could say would convince them I had nothing to do with the tragedy. So I am banished from the family circle. If it were not for the fact that you are now so securely within it, I should not care."

He caught Valeria once again in his arms.

"But I do care because you are the most beautiful woman I know and you have to be mine – *all mine.*"

Valeria desired nothing more than to sink into his arms and allow him to kiss her into oblivion, but a small, stern voice within her told her that this was not right, not without being engaged.

"I am not your plaything, sir," she insisted firmly, forcing herself to step out of the circle of his arms.

He looked at her with unsettling intensity.

"I shall show you just what a plaything you are and how you will enjoy the games I play."

Whatever she felt, this was too much for Valeria.

"I suggest you leave now, sir."

He gave her a long look.

"You need not think you can escape me," he said finally, his voice throaty and passionate. "You will be in London for the Jubilee – and indeed so shall I. We shall meet again. In the meantime, *remember me!*"

Suddenly she was once again swept up in his arms and into another passionate kiss.

With a small cry Valeria disentangled herself.

Every pulse in her body throbbed from the impact of his assault and cried out for more.

Her few wits fought against her emotions.

"I hope I never see you again," she shouted.

Then she turned round and ran as fast as she could back towards The Castle.

As soon as she was safely on the drawbridge, she stopped and drew deep reviving breaths.

Away from the pulsating presence of Sir Peter, she could tell herself that no gentleman of any honour would behave in the way he did – Lord Waterford never would.

She was very relieved that their meeting could not have been seen from The Castle.

Suddenly something inside her so wished that Lord Waterford could make her feel the way Sir Peter did.

*

Nothing else occurred to disturb Valeria before she left for Richmond and her beloved home.

As soon as she arrived home, her Papa told her that he too had been invited to join them at Waterford House.

"However," he said with a wicked look in his eye, "I thanked him, but had to decline his very kind invitation as I had already accepted another."

"Papa! Where are you going?"

"Lady Braithwaite has asked me to join her party. You were included in the invitation, but I explained that you were otherwise engaged. You will remember Lady Braithwaite?" he added, a little anxiously.

It took her a moment or two to recall an attractive widow who was part of her father's Social circle.

"I do, Papa. And I like her very much. I shall not tease you, but will await further developments with happy anticipation!"

Despite her words, however, Valeria felt unhappy. However charming no woman could take the place of her dearest Mama.

"Now, now! Cast such thoughts from your mind! My darling girl, I have no intention of marrying again. It is just that Maria and I have a comfortable understanding."

Valeria immediately felt happier.

Then her Papa remarked,

"Now you are going to stay at Waterford House, I feel that I should be looking forward to the announcement of your engagement."

"Papa! There is no such understanding with Lord Waterford. I am merely helping him to restore his Castle."

He refused to be put off. He placed a finger beside his nose in a gesture of complicity and muttered,

"Quite, quite, my dear. I fully understand."

"Papa, I think that Lord Waterford has changed his mind over wanting to offer for me."

"Has he said so?"

"Not in so many words. But – it's rather difficult to explain – it is just that I don't think he trusts me anymore."

Even as she said it, Valeria realised how much the thought hurt.

"Of course he trusts you. My daughter would not behave in any sort of way that could make him doubt her."

Valeria gave up.

Nothing would make her Papa understand. She did not want to mention Sir Peter.

After all, Lord Waterford could have no idea how

his kisses made her feel. Nor could she explain that she felt guilty every time she remembered those kisses.

As she travelled to London, Valeria was nervous.

She was wondering what her relationship with Lord Waterford would be away from his Castle. There they had seemed to share a purpose. In London there would be so many distractions.

When she arrived at Waterford House in Park Lane, Valeria was intensely disappointed to find that neither Lord Waterford nor Susan was at home.

"His Lordship and her Ladyship will return soon," intoned the butler. "Tea is served in the drawing room."

Later she was taken into a bedroom that looked out onto a garden and graceful trees.

There was, however, nothing rural about Waterford House itself. Everything about it breathed an entrancing mix of elegance and comfort.

Then Lord Waterford arrived and was concerned to find out if Valeria had been properly received.

He seemed rather distant.

With a sense of depression, Valeria became certain that he no longer wanted her as his wife.

Susan appeared delighted to see Valeria and swept her into the same friendship they had had at The Castle.

From then on there hardly seemed a spare moment.

Susan seemed determined that the ball was to be the success of the Season and every aspect of the arrangements had her full attention.

Valeria herself was involved with tracking down a vast number of items she deemed essential for The Castle.

This did not interfere in any way with her attending all the luncheons, receptions, dinners and balls that Susan, Lord Waterford and she were invited to.

It seemed everyone in London wanted to celebrate the sixtieth anniversary of Queen Victoria's accession to the Throne.

As Lord Waterford claimed a dance from Valeria at the first ball they attended, he murmured,

"I don't know how many trunks you brought with you, but this is one of the loveliest gowns I have ever seen. Or perhaps it is that the wearer makes it look so."

Her heart raced at this unexpected compliment.

He had seemed so offhand since she had arrived at Waterford House, such a compliment now was disturbing.

She smiled at him.

"It was one that I chose for Juliette's engagement celebrations. I am so glad you like it, my Lord."

"Ah! Now I do remember it, but I failed to see the gown, it was the girl who wore it who was so captivating!"

Another compliment!

Valeria's heart thudded in a very unfamiliar way.

Could it be that Lord Waterford was still interested in renewing his suit?

If so, could she bring herself to accept it? Was she now prepared to accept his offer of marriage founded on friendship rather than passion?

Lord Waterford said nothing else as he guided her round the floor. His hand in the small of her back felt very protective and Valeria for once was content not to indulge in frivolous chit-chat with her partner.

Instead she let the music and the movement of their bodies spirit her away from the crowds and into a glorious space that only they inhabited.

At the end of the dance Lord Waterford looked into her eyes and said in a quiet voice,

"Thank you, Miss Montford, that was – " he left the end of the sentence hanging in the air as a young man came up eager to claim Valeria for the next dance.

She was in demand for every dance.

She had hoped that Lord Waterford would take her into the buffet, but when there was a break in the music, he was then chatting with Lady Mere, a married beauty with a reputation for fast living.

She was not someone Valeria expected to attract Lord Waterford. She was exceedingly attractive and he did seem to be enjoying her company in a way that suggested they were completely at ease with each other.

Lord Mere, she knew, was elderly and never went out in Society and there was gossip about his young wife's flirtations.

Was Lord Waterford her latest conquest?

Then, at the other end of the ballroom, Valeria saw a sleek blond head rising above the figures around him.

Her heart lifted.

Next Valeria's Papa appeared in a jovial mood.

"I saw you take the floor with Charles Waterford," he murmured. "Lovely couple you make."

"Hush, Papa," responded Valeria nervously.

"Have you decided to accept him yet?"

"Papa!"

"I thought that was the idea for you to be staying at Waterford House. Of course!" he exclaimed as though a sudden revelation had hit him. "The announcement will be made at the Waterford Ball. Quite right, too."

"Papa," Valeria scolded him sternly. "Stop talking like this. Don't you remember what I told you?"

She felt very strange.

Had it been any other man she had danced with in such an intimate fashion as she had with Lord Waterford, she would have been convinced that he was madly in love with her.

But Lord Waterford was not any other man.

He hid his feelings so expertly that two unexpected compliments and his way of moving with her as though they inhabited one body could mean nothing.

"There you are, Christopher! And with Valeria, how lovely!"

Lady Braithwaite then slipped her hand through Sir Christopher's arm.

"Valeria, my dear, I do hope that you and both the Waterfords will be coming to my *Thé Dansant* next week."

Valeria summoned a smile.

"The acceptances were sent out this morning, Lady Braithwaite. It should be a delightful occasion."

Lady Braithwaite gave her a complicit smile.

"And it will be delightful to have you all there. So splendid to see you so happily settled in Waterford House."

"I am fulfilling my commission connected with the restoration of Waterford Castle," Valeria told her as calmly as she could manage.

"Of course, my dear. I quite understand."

But she knew Lady Braithwaite's understanding of the situation was exactly the same as her father's.

Her heart sank.

"Now, I am going to snatch dear Christopher away. I wish him to meet some old friends from the North."

Valeria watched them walk away feeling despair.

They both seemed convinced that Lord Waterford wanted her to be his wife.

"So, this is where you have hidden yourself is it?"

Sir Peter stood in front of Valeria.

He gave her one of his most wicked smiles. It was the sort of smile that made her think that he could see right through her clothes to her naked body.

She felt herself flush and she was filled with sudden anger. She wondered what he wanted. He told her he was consumed with passion for her, yet he made no move that suggested he was ready to make her an offer of marriage.

In fact, she suddenly realised, he behaved as though his intentions towards her were quite different.

How could he possibly raise such wayward feelings in her and not behave with propriety?

Valeria's anger grew.

With a single skilful movement, Sir Peter tweaked her dance programme and pencil off her arm.

She thanked the fates that it was completely filled. There was no dance available for Sir Peter.

Sir Peter scratched off a couple of names, wrote in his own and handed the programme back to her.

"There now," he crowed with an arrogant look that burned into her. "We shall draw all eyes."

"How dare you!"

Valeria's anger spilled over.

She dug the pencil into the programme, obliterating his name.

"You have no right!"

His teeth gleamed as his smile broadened.

"Oh, I have every right," he cooed softly. "You will be mine. I know it and you know it."

It sounded as though it might just be a proposal of marriage, but Valeria knew with absolute certainty that it was not.

"You are mistaken, sir," she retorted stiffly and left him standing there as she rejoined her partner.

As she took up her plate of food, she could feel Sir Peter's eyes boring into her back.

She refused to turn around.

A little later an acquaintance brought up Lady Mere to be introduced to her.

"I had to meet the girl who has been doing so much to restore Waterford Castle," she said and looked at Valeria with interest. "Charles and I are *such* close friends – "

Valeria thought she heard a particular emphasis on the last words and understood exactly what her Ladyship intended to convey.

"Indeed," she said, taking an instant dislike to her.

She softly touched her wrist with her fan.

"We must have a long chat, you and I, sometime. But not now, I think."

A moment later she was snatched away by her other friends and Valeria was relieved to see her go.

She was not sure what Lady Mere meant that they needed a long chat, but she was certain it would not be to her, Valeria's, advantage.

Towards the end of the interval, Lord Waterford appeared at her side. He looked concerned.

"Miss Montford, I am so sorry, my sister is feeling unwell. I need to take her home. We do not want to spoil your evening and Lady Braithwaite is happy to act as your chaperone instead of Susan."

Valeria knew at once what she wanted to do.

"Lord Waterford, it is so kind of Lady Braithwaite, but I would prefer to accompany Susan home. Poor Susan must be feeling sad to leave and I would worry about her and have no pleasure if I remain while she goes home."

His face immediately lightened.

"How very good of you, Miss Montford."

Susan was sitting in the hall, her face very pale and she held a hand to her eyes.

It did not take long for Valeria to find their wraps and to assure Susan that she much preferred going with her than staying at the ball.

"There are very many balls over the next few weeks that to shorten this one is nothing," she assured her. "Please tell me how you feel."

She put out a hand to help her to the door.

"It is merely a sudden headache. But it was so hot I felt that if I remained a moment longer, I would collapse. Oh, isn't the night air refreshing?"

As they stood on the top step of the porch, waiting for their coach, a tall man with blond hair hurried down the steps past them.

Susan suddenly grabbed at Valeria's arm, gripping it so hard, Valeria almost cried out.

The young man turned and waved at a coach down on the road.

Susan's hand relaxed.

In a moment of blinding insight, Valeria realised that she had thought he might be Sir Peter.

Could his appearance at the ball be the reason for Susan's sudden headache? Had she flirted with him before the death of her husband? Was that the reason Sir John had accepted the racing challenge that had ended so tragically?

"Is your headache worse, Susan?" Valeria asked, looking round for Lord Waterford.

"Oh, no. It is fine, thank you," she murmured.

"Here is the carriage now," called Lord Waterford,

reappearing at that moment and helping in first Susan and then Valeria.

Valeria sank back in the carriage with a feeling of deep relief.

For once she did not mind leaving a ball early. The thought of having to deal with Sir Peter claiming her for dances already promised would be too much – particularly when she thought how Lord Waterford would react.

Valeria accompanied Susan up to her room and saw her safely into the protective arms of her elderly maid.

Afterwards, rather than going to her own bedroom, she returned downstairs with a vague idea of sharing a chat and perhaps a glass of wine with Lord Waterford.

She wondered where he would be.

Valeria tried the salon where they would gather if no guests were present.

It was empty.

So tried the drawing room, but it too was empty.

Then Valeria noticed that the French doors out onto the terrace were slightly ajar.

Moving across the room, she arrived in the garden just in time to see Lord Waterford disappearing through the garden gate that led into the Park.

Where could he be going?

CHAPTER EIGHT

Valeria could only think that he had arranged an assignation with someone.

She recalled the intimate way he had spoken with Lady Mere and then mused about her reputation.

Could he be going to visit her? Could Lady Mere actually be waiting for him in Green Park?

She was conscious of a sick feeling in her stomach.

Wishing she had gone to bed, she went upstairs.

All the time she was trying to give Mary, her maid, a lively account of the evening, Valeria could not banish the picture in her mind of the pretty and effervesant Lady Mere talking with a seemingly enraptured Lord Waterford.

It took her a long time to fall asleep that night.

*

The days leading up to Queen Victoria's Jubilee Celebrations grew more and more filled with activity.

Susan recovered from her headache overnight and there was no recurrence.

But Valeria noted that Sir Peter did not attend any of the other functions they had been invited to.

She did not know whether she should be relieved or disappointed.

What concerned her more was looking out to see if Lady Mere was present and, if so, would Lord Waterford be dancing with her?

Twice Valeria noticed her, looking more attractive than ever at every ball and several times she did see Lord Waterford dancing with her.

Quite soon she became aware that Society appeared to take for granted that an engagement between her and Lord Waterford would be announced at the Waterford Ball.

Too late she realised that she had made an error in accepting his invitation to stay at Waterford House.

Susan's presence meant that the arrangement was perfectly respectable, but if no engagement emerged at the end of the Jubilee Celebrations, Society would assume that she herself had been found wanting or draw the conclusion that she had turned Lord Waterford down. In either event her reputation would be badly damaged.

For Valeria this was the least of her worries.

*

Standing at her window one night after yet another ball, Valeria suddenly saw Lord Waterford emerge from the drawing room windows.

He walked into the garden and left through the gate into the Park. In a moment he was swallowed up by the darkness of the trees.

It was as if pincers had seized hold of her heart and tightened around it.

He must be on his way to another assignation with the seductive Lady Mere.

Valeria sank into a chair, her head in her hands.

After a moment she straightened and told herself to forget what she had seen.

After all it was only Lord Waterford's business.

She already realised he was no longer interested in making her his wife. And had she not refused to consider marrying him anyway?

It was quite easy enough to tell herself this, more difficult to slip into sleep.

In the morning she looked at Lord Waterford as if he was a new species that had just been discovered.

She saw his courtesy towards his sister, twittering in a distressed manner over some detail of the buffet for the Waterford Ball that was now to be held on the very night that Queen Victoria's Jubilee was celebrated.

When Valeria gently intervened with a suggestion that a Yorkshire pie might be introduced into the menu, she gloried in Lord Waterford's quick look of appreciation.

"A Yorkshire pie? What, pray, Valeria, is that?"

"Why it is a boned goose or turkey, stuffed with a boned duck, then with a chicken, ending up with whatever small bird can be found. The slices of differently shaded meats make a most unusual effect."

Susan clapped her hands together.

"You are so clever, Valeria! Charles, don't you think that sounds quite the thing?"

Lord Waterford smiled.

"I do. And I agree with you that Miss Montford is indeed clever."

Valeria found herself blushing.

"Charles, Valeria means to visit textile shops this morning to choose suitable items for The Castle. You will accompany us?" suggested Susan.

"What?" He then started in what to Valeria seemed a guilty manner. "No, I am afraid I have other business on today. I am sure you do not need my advice anyway."

Suddenly for no very good reason, Valeria recalled the deserted house on the Waterford estate for which Lord Waterford had refused to declare his plans.

What if he was planning to use it for assignations with the Lady Mere?

Maybe even to install her there?

Perhaps this morning he was planning to meet her in some safely public place to make the final arrangements.

"This is the last task I need to undertake," Valeria said in a tone that was almost a challenge, "everything else I need to find for the interior decoration of your Castle has already been ordered."

"Excellent," he remarked, but he sounded offhand.

Valeria felt a sense of defeat.

No one had said anything about her accompanying Lord Waterford and Susan when they returned to his Castle after the Jubilee Celebrations.

Susan seemed to take it for granted that she would, but Valeria knew that the invitation had to come from Lord Waterford.

He had said nothing.

She was astonished at how bleak the thought was that she would not be returning to The Castle.

Lord Waterford stood up.

"I wish you success with your morning's errand. I look forward to seeing you in time for the Berkeley Square Reception we are invited to this evening."

Valeria watched his lean and casually elegant figure disappear, surprised at the depth of her disappointment that she would not have his company again until that evening.

As she waited in the hallway of Waterford House for Susan to join her, her mind was torn with emotion.

Had she, in spite of her initial antagonism, begun to fall in love with Lord Waterford?

Surely not.

Where were the waves of passion for Sir Peter?

No, her feelings for Lord Waterford were for a man whose companionship she had learned to enjoy.

She admired his intelligent conversation, quiet wit and his sympathetic way of ensuring that life ran smoothly for those he cared about.

"Valeria, my dear, *disaster!*" Susan appeared all of a fluster. "The chef is inspired by your idea of Yorkshire pie and now insists on discussing other delights with me urgently this morning."

"Never mind, Susan, I can easily do it on my own."

"But no footman can be spared to accompany you, nor any maid. Making sure the house is ready to entertain so many tomorrow is taking every pair of hands available."

"Perhaps I should not take your carriage, then, I can find a hansom cab, I'm sure."

Susan was shocked.

"My dear, of course not! It is bad enough that you have to go alone."

"Nonsense, I only have the one destination, it could not be simpler. I will soon be back here, my work done."

"You are so efficient, Valeria," murmured Susan, "I look forward to your return."

Valeria went out to the waiting carriage.

She did not notice the figure of a man a little way down the street, half hidden behind another carriage.

As her carriage paused to take its place in the *mêlée* of traffic in St. James's Street, the man then flagged down a passing hansom cab and gave instructions to follow.

Arriving at the shop, she told the coachman when to return. She had allowed enough time not to be rushed, but she finished her ordering earlier than she had expected.

She had noticed some interesting-looking shops as she had arrived, so she then decided, despite the lack of a chaperone, to have a look.

No sooner had she emerged into the street than her wrist was seized.

"*Now I have you,*" crowed Sir Peter Cousins.

Shocked, astonished, and immediately realising that she was not at all pleased to see him, Valeria attempted to pull her arm away.

"Let me go," she cried. "How dare you accost me."

But she found herself pulled around a corner into a narrow side street. At its far end was a Church surrounded by a small graveyard.

"Here we can talk," Sir Peter hissed, his voice tense as he dragged her towards the graveyard.

Valeria opened her mouth to scream, then closed it as she thought of the scandal that would ensue if anyone did come to her aid.

After all Sir Peter might just want to talk to her.

Still trying to break free from him she found herself helpless in his strong grip.

The churchyard was deserted.

Inside its tall iron gate, Sir Peter released his hold on her, only to pull her straight back into his arms and kiss her passionately.

Despite her initial horror at his attack, a familiar hunger began to run through her veins that swept away her frustration at the loss of Lord Waterford's courtship.

At least Sir Peter said that he was in love with her and if he lacked Lord Waterford's courtesy and kindness, the fact that he loved her surely made up for these defects.

"Oh, Valeria," Sir Peter sighed, raising his mouth at last from hers. "How I have longed for this moment. The days I have hung around Waterford House hoping to see you emerge without a keeper!

"And now I have you, I am not going to let you go. You are the most tantalising, gorgeous creature I have ever known. My gambler's soul yearns for you."

Valeria gazed into his dark eyes, her heart beating erratically.

"You mean we shall be married?" she breathed.

Suddenly he dropped his arms.

"*Marriage!*" He gave out a high-pitched scornful laugh. "What on earth gave you that idea?"

She staggered with the suddenness of her release and the fire in her veins turned to ice.

"I – don't understand," she stammered. "You – said you loved me!"

"I said I wanted you, that I longed for you. You do things to me no other woman has ever done. There is some terrible magic in your eyes, your mouth, your body."

Valeria was filled with sudden anticipation.

"Why, then – surely you would wish to marry me?"

"Oh," he added with a touch of desperation. "Had you money, had you a large fortune, why then, yes, I would marry you like a shot."

"Money! Is that all you can think of?"

"I cannot afford to marry a bride without wealth."

"*Lord Waterford can.*"

The words were out without any thought.

"Ha!" His eyes glittered. "So, you have intentions in that direction, do you?"

"Lord Waterford – "

Valeria started, then paused, trying to make sense of the situation she found herself in. But her mind was like a mouse going round and round in a tiny wheel, unable to find a way out.

Sir Peter leant against the fence, a sneer on his face.

"Waterford is a devious hypocrite. Do not believe him if he says he loves you. Have you not seen the way he sneaks out of the back gate of his mansion late at night to assignations with his mistress?"

Valeria unconsciously put a hand to her breast.

Her heart was beating so fast she thought she would fall senseless to the ground.

So, it was true!

Sir Peter's sneer vanished.

He drew her to him again.

"Give up all thoughts of Waterford. He can never make you happy the way I can."

Valeria pulled away, the abruptness of her move taking Sir Peter by surprise.

"You disgust me," she raged. "You accuse Lord Waterford of deviousness yet you expect me to come away with you like – like – a floosie! You have no honour, sir."

She ran through the churchyard gate, pulling it shut behind her with a clang.

By the time Sir Peter managed to open it again, Valeria had reached the street and run back into the shop.

The assistant immediately came forward.

She took a deep breath.

A few moments later the Waterford coach arrived and she then walked steadily out of the shop, not glancing to right or left as she stepped into the carriage.

As she sank back onto the buttoned cushions, she felt as though she had been pushed through a wringer like a piece of washed clothing.

All the exciting emotions that being kissed by Sir Peter aroused in her had vanished.

The very thought of him filled her with disgust and even to think of the excitement she felt in his arms made her feel degraded.

All he wanted was to make her his mistress! How could she ever have imagined they could be man and wife?

Then she recalled how he called Lord Waterford a 'devious hypocrite'.

Sir Peter must have been in Green Park watching Waterford House night after night.

How, she wondered, could she ever have thought the man attractive? How had he managed to arouse her so profoundly?

Valeria had no answer to these questions. She could only blame herself for being so misled by him.

She suddenly felt very humble.

She remembered her initial dislike, hatred even, for Lord Waterford. That was because he made her feel less than the woman she was convinced she was.

Now she was beginning to feel deflated because she had overestimated her own worth.

She had been convinced that Sir Peter loved her and would ask her to marry him. Instead he had professed that without any money she was nothing more than a desirable object for his bed!

The fact that he had stirred her responses in a way no other man ever had only made it worse. How could she have been so shallow as to fall for a man merely because of his physical attractions?

No wonder Lord Waterford had decided he was no longer interested in marrying her!

Next she must face his assignations.

It just had to be true. Lord Waterford had actually met his love in Green Park, hidden amongst the leafy trees.

It was a most thoroughly despondent Valeria who alighted from the carriage at Waterford House and thanked the coachman.

She looked up at the steps leading to the front door and wondered whether she should leave and return home.

Then she remembered that her father was staying with Lady Braithwaite and their house had been closed up until after the Jubilee.

Also she knew that Susan was relying on her help with tomorrow's ball.

Finally the thought of never seeing Lord Waterford again was suddenly more than she could bear.

Soon their relationship would be at an end, but in the meantime she wanted to enjoy a last dance with him.

Valeria mounted the steps determined to be at her most captivating until she actually left Waterford House.

*

Prepared to report on her morning's work to Lord Waterford, Valeria found that he had disappeared.

He did not appear for luncheon and, when Valeria and Susan were ready to leave for Berkeley Square, a note arrived from Lord Waterford presenting his regrets that he was unable to accompany them to the Reception.

"Arriving without an escort is too, too degrading," Susan huffed despairingly. "How will I ever live it down?"

Valeria's spirits fell lower than ever.

The Reception went smoothly. Their hostess only raised one eyebrow as Susan gave her brother's apologies.

"A shame, but never mind. But we look forward so much to your ball tomorrow night," she murmured, leaning forward to kiss Susan's cheek and then offering her hand to Valeria. "It will be the event of the Season."

Susan lamented all the way home that expectations of their ball were running far too high.

Valeria tried to comfort her.

"You have made the very best arrangements anyone could. It will be a triumph."

"You will do the flowers tomorrow morning before we go to the St. Paul's ceremony?"

"Of course I will," Valeria assured her.

*

The flowers and three florists arrived very early in the morning. Valeria was all ready for them and soon they were hard at work.

"Oh," exclaimed Susan later, arriving just as the last flowers were secured in place. "It all looks perfect."

Valeria agreed that the effect was magical, but she could not help feeling sad.

Tonight's ball would mark the end of her friendship with Lord Waterford and she was slowly becoming aware that he had captured her heart.

Without realising it she had fallen in love with him!

"Come," called out Susan, "we must leave for St. Paul's."

Valeria went to her room to dress herself for the big occasion and chose her most stunning afternoon gown with a matching hat.

A quick glance in the mirror soon confirmed that her appearance should please even the fiercest critic.

As she came downstairs, Lord Waterford walked over to her.

"You look wonderful," he breathed, then he turned

to his sister. "I am the luckiest of men to be accompanied by the two most beautiful women in the whole country!"

Valeria felt an extraordinary lifting of her heart.

The look in his eyes could almost convince her that he *did* still wish to marry her.

She allowed him to hand her into the carriage and his touch on her arm seemed to burn into her flesh.

All through the journey through the crowded streets to St. Paul's Cathedral, Valeria was aware of nothing else but Lord Waterford sitting opposite in the open carriage.

"I feel quite like a Queen myself," laughed Susan, waving at the crowds lining the Strand and Fleet Street as they cheered the long line of carriages.

Valeria laughed with her, but her attention was for Lord Waterford who pointed out sights of interest.

He had secured for them seats in one of the stands overlooking the steps of St. Paul's.

The Queen's arrival was preceded with parades of Cavalry and endless Highlanders proudly playing bagpipes until Susan said she would scream with the noise.

Later all Valeria found she could remember was the sound of cheers gradually growing louder as the Queen's open carriage came into view. Her Majesty was dressed in grey and black and looked quite composed, holding a long-handled black lace parasol.

The Service was held in the open air, the Queen all the time sitting in her carriage, too frail to climb the steps.

"Such a minute figure to represent the might of the British Empire," murmured Lord Waterford into Valeria's ear as the ceremony drew to a close.

She turned to him eagerly.

"I was thinking exactly the same!"

"You were?"

His eyes met hers and there was something in them that made her blush. She could feel the colour rising up her neck to her face.

She was rescued by a mighty cheer that went up as the Queen's carriage moved forward to begin the journey back to Buckingham Palace.

*

On their return to Waterford House, arrangements for the ball claimed all Valeria's attention. Between all the details that needed checking and trying to soothe Susan's nerves, she seemed to have no opportunity to spend time with Lord Waterford.

Finally Valeria went to dress.

"Oh, miss, you do look wonderful," enthused Mary, when she was ready.

There were white roses in Valeria's hair, she was wearing a white silk dress with gathered and puffed sleeves that left her shoulders bare.

More roses were placed between her breasts. Long white gloves and white silk shoes completed her ensemble.

Valeria hoped that Lord Waterford would admire her appearance as much as Mary did.

She picked up a white lace fan, thanked her maid for her help and left her bedroom.

Downstairs, she saw Lord Waterford waiting in the hall. But instead of looking up to see her descend, he was reading a note he had just been handed. Whatever the note contained, it obviously pleased him as his face lit up.

Then Susan joined Valeria on the stairs and called to her brother. He stuffed the note into the pocket of his dress trousers and looked up.

"How beautiful you both are," he murmured softly as they descended.

"You look so distinguished tonight, Charles dear," cooed Susan, taking his arm as she reached his side.

Valeria envied her, she would have liked so much to have felt able to slip her hand through his other arm.

As she followed them into the drawing room, she could not help wondering what the contents of the note had been. Was it to arrange another assignation after the ball?

The question nagged at her all evening, even when Lord Waterford claimed a waltz from her.

"Your ball is a great success," Valeria said as he skilfully steered her round the floor.

He gave her the smile that she always thought held great sweetness.

"You have helped Susan so much. If it is a success tonight, much of the credit must go to you."

Valeria glowed.

She could not bring herself to conduct the sort of light conversation that was expected at such affairs.

She just wanted above all to ask him if he intended renewing his suit, but that was such an impossible subject to raise at this or indeed any other moment.

Maybe if he asked her to return with him and Susan to The Castle, she would be able to gauge whether he still wanted to marry her.

Meanwhile, she said nothing, glorying in the close contact with him as he swept her round the floor.

He was a marvellous dancer, the music seemed to flow through him and through his hands into Valeria.

When the last strains of the waltz faded, she stood breathing quickly beside him as they clapped the orchestra.

"Thank you," Lord Waterford said and, again, his eyes seemed to say what his lips were not prepared to utter.

"I see your next partner is coming to snatch you away," he declared as a young man came up eagerly.

"And you must claim your next partner too."

His hand rested on her arm for a moment, as though he would have liked to take her away into a quiet corner.

It was not to be.

The evening was an enormous success. Everyone was talking about the Service at St. Paul's Cathedral that morning and how fitting it was they should be attending such a wonderful ball.

But for Valeria, the evening was bittersweet.

There was no other opportunity to dance with Lord Waterford. Instead she watched him dance with a series of women, including Lady Mere, who seemed in scintillating form, whispering into his ear as he danced closely with her.

Valeria then tore her gaze away and concentrated on entertaining her partner.

Gradually she sensed that many of the guests were waiting for an announcement of Lord Waterford's and her engagement.

As the evening drew towards a close, the whispers grew louder.

Now they appeared to express disappointment and many eyes were turned on Valeria.

Her cheeks burning, she still held her head high and flirted determinedly with young men she found boring.

She wished so much for the end of the evening.

It was well into the early hours before she was able to retreat to her bedroom.

Mary was waiting to help her out of her clothes and she was avid for a description of every aspect of the ball.

As soon as her dress had been unfastened, however, Valeria sent her to bed, promising to give her a complete account the next day.

At last she was on her own.

Starting to brush her hair, Valeria wandered over to the window, looking out at Green Park.

Then to her consternation she saw Lord Waterford walk steadily down the garden to the gate into the Park.

It was as though a knife had been stuck in her heart.

Hardly knowing what she was doing, she pulled on the nearest day dress, slipped into a pair of pumps, hastily tied her hair back and then flew down the stairs without a sound.

There were no servants in the hall or in the drawing room as she ran out onto the terrace and down to the gate.

Valeria was determined to find out the truth about Lord Waterford's assignations.

CHAPTER NINE

The night air was warm, but clouds obscured any moonlight.

At the gate leading into the Park, Valeria paused, trying to adjust her eyes to the darkness.

She was aware of the tall pine trees and the rustle of their leaves all around her but little else.

Then, as she stood by the open gate, she began to see figures, obviously tramps, lying on the grass, some on newspapers, others with cardboard laid over their bodies.

They all seemed to be asleep.

But where was Lord Waterford?

Had he walked across the Park and into Piccadilly? Had he been heading for Lady Mere's house?

Then, suddenly, Valeria saw him.

Even through the murky gloom, the outline of his figure was unmistakeable.

Lord Waterford was no more than just a few dozen yards away from her and, instead of embracing Lady Mere, he seemed to be bending down over one of the down-and-outs lying on the grass.

She shrank back against the gate, afraid he would look up and spot the pale glow of her dress.

Instead to her horror she saw a figure approaching Lord Waterford with a cudgel raised at his head.

She instantly screamed out a warning.

Lord Waterford looked up, but a savage blow felled him to the ground.

Shouting for help, Valeria ran forward and then saw two tramps weigh into the attacker with their fists.

He was very tall and looked strong but such was the ferocity of the assault, he backed away from the doughty fighters. Valeria realised that his head was covered in an all-embracing hood that hid any identifying features.

Ignoring the fight, she flung herself onto the ground beside Lord Waterford's horrifyingly still figure.

She tried to turn him, but his weight was too great.

She ran her fingers over the back of his head – his hair felt damp and sticky whilst his breathing was heavy and intermittent.

She looked around desperately for help.

The recumbent figures were stirring, roused by the grunts of the fight. Several went to join in, others melted away into the darkness.

Faced with a growing number to contend with, the attacker suddenly broke away with a curse and ran towards Piccadilly.

Valeria longed to run for help, but feared to leave Lord Waterford unprotected.

At that moment two footmen appeared at the gate equipped with flaming torches.

"Over here," Valeria called out. "Come quickly."

The footmen hurried over, their torches lighting a path through the darkness. They were in shirtsleeves, no time had been lost donning their usual gold-braided livery.

"Lord Waterford has been viciously attacked and he is unconscious," Valeria gasped as they approached.

She suddenly became aware of how very strange it

all must seem to them – Lord Waterford lying senseless in the Park, she kneeling beside him.

"We heard you scream, miss," volunteered John, the elder of the two footmen.

"Thank Heavens. Now hold your torches over here so that I can see how badly his Lordship has been hurt."

She made a quick intake of breath as she saw the blood pouring from a wound at the back of his head. She looked at her hands and they, too, were covered in blood.

For a moment Valeria had to close her eyes.

She fought with herself not to swoon, then looked up at the footmen.

"You will need to bring a stretcher to carry Lord Waterford back to the house. And a doctor must be sent for immediately."

"Who attacked his Lordship, miss?" asked the other footman.

"I don't know, Martin," she replied distractedly.

She looked around for the two down-and-outs who had come to Lord Waterford's aid, but they had vanished.

"Go, please!" she instructed the footmen. "No, one of you stay here with me. Whoever it was who attacked him could return. The torchlight should keep us safe."

Then, heedless of any propriety, she lifted her skirt and, using her teeth, tore a strip off the end of her petticoat.

She folded the strip into two and, her heart in her mouth, applied the strip round the dreadful wound on Lord Waterford's bleeding head.

John held the torch high. An intake of breath from him underlined the seriousness of the wound.

As soon as the bandage was wound round his head, it reddened with blood.

Valeria became frantic to have him removed from the scene back into the house.

"Why are they taking so long?"

"I'm sure, miss, Martin is going just as quick as he can," said John. "We all thinks the world of his Lordship. If there's anything we can do to help, we'll be doing it, you can be sure of that!"

Valeria believed him.

She took hold of Lord Waterford's hand.

It felt cold and clammy. She tried to find his pulse, but its erratic beat frightened her, so she just held his hand.

Eventually a team of servants, most of them only half dressed, came running over the garden carrying a door.

Among them was the butler, the only one properly dressed. He organised the gentle lifting of Lord Waterford onto the door.

The wounded man groaned as they lifted him.

"*Careful,*" cautioned Valeria.

She took hold of his hand again as they raised the door and its load from the ground.

Awkwardly the little group carried Lord Waterford through the French windows and into the house.

"Where to, Miss Montford?" asked the butler.

"Can you carry his Lordship up to his bedroom?"

"Of course, miss."

The stairs had to be taken slowly. Valeria followed closely behind, terrified that they would let Lord Waterford slip off the door.

But somehow the little team managed to carry him up the stairs and into his bedroom.

George, Lord Waterford's valet, took a towel from the washstand and placed it on the bed and then his body was lifted as gently as they could onto the bed.

There came a thunderous knock on the door.

"That will be Doctor Marshall," said the butler and left the room.

He was a small busy-looking man who appeared to have dressed hastily.

Doctor Marshall crossed to the bed, surveyed his patient and tutted under his breath as he took in the ghastly whiteness of Lord Waterford's face, the heavy breathing, and the closed eyes.

Placing a hand on the bandage, he enquired,

"Who applied this?"

"I did, sir," volunteered Valeria, "I saw him hit on the head and when I saw the way blood was pouring from his scalp, I had to do something."

Her gaze then returned to Lord Waterford's face. It looked so white and pinched, as though he was preparing to depart this life.

"Will he be all right, doctor?"

His kind eyes looked at her closely for a moment.

"I need to examine him," he replied briefly. "Do I address Lady Waterford?"

Valeria blushed deeply and shook her head.

"I am Miss Montford. I am a guest here."

The doctor gave a little nod of his head.

"I shall need two bowls of warm water, some clean towels and shaving gear."

Two footmen and George disappeared.

The doctor asked for help in turning the wounded man so that he could examine the injury to the back of his head and the butler assisted him.

Undoing Valeria's bandage, the doctor asked,

"Has Lady Stratfield been informed of her brother's injury?"

Valeria looked at the butler, who shook his head.

"It should be done."

The butler looked anything but willing to undertake this task.

"Shall I?" asked Valeria, trying not to see the mess of blood and tangled hair that removing the bandage had revealed.

"If you would be so kind, Miss Montford."

Susan was fast asleep.

Valeria gently shook her shoulder.

Susan opened her eyes, stared uncomprehendingly for a moment, then pulled herself up in bed.

"What can have happened? Why are you dressed like that, Valeria?"

Her voice was sharp and anxious.

Using as few words as possible, Valeria told her all that had happened.

Susan shrieked.

And then shrieked again.

"No, no, no! It can't be so. Tell me it isn't so."

Valeria sat on the bed and hugged her.

"I am afraid it is so, Susan, dearest."

"And he might die, you say?"

"Doctor Marshall has to examine him before he can say how serious the injury is. Will you not come along to your brother's bedside and see him for yourself?"

Susan shrank back in her bed.

"I can't," she whimpered, waving her hands around in front of her face. "Don't ask me. I cannot bear blood.

Really, I cannot. Oh, God," her voice rose again. "I just cannot bear it if he dies – "

She collapsed onto her pillows crying hysterically.

Valeria sat with her for a few minutes, stroking her hand and trying to soothe her. But her mind was back in that other bedroom with Lord Waterford.

Soon she could not bear not to be there, so she rose.

"I will find your maid and send her to you, Susan, but I have to go back to your brother."

Susan moaned.

"Send me news. Send that he will be all right. He *must* be all right."

Valeria returned to Lord Waterford's room and then approached the bed.

Beside it was a bowl of reddened water and another full of locks of bloody hair and flecks of shaving cream.

The doctor was finishing bandaging his head.

Lord Waterford's face remained terrifyingly white and his breathing still resembled snoring.

The doctor then stood back from the bed, picked up a clean towel and wiped his hands.

"Does Lady Stratfield come to her brother's side, Miss Montford?" he asked, waving one of the footmen to remove the two bowls.

"I am afraid that she's too upset to come. Can you please tell me how Lord Waterford is?"

The doctor's jacket had been discarded and now he started to roll down the sleeves of his shirt.

"We need to undress him," he addressed the butler. He turned to Valeria. "Since Lady Stratfield cannot attend her brother, Miss Montford, if you will wait downstairs, I will report to you as soon as his Lordship is settled."

Valeria took a last lingering look at his pinched and pale face.

His heavy breathing seemed to follow her as she walked slowly downstairs full of trepidation.

Soup and brandy had been laid on in the morning room and, despite the fact that it was a mild summer night, a fire had been lit.

Valeria sat huddled beside the flames and sipped the soup, trying to warm herself.

When the doctor entered the room, she jumped up.

"How is he?" she asked him urgently.

The doctor made a vague movement with his hand. He looked tired and defeated.

Her heart in her mouth, Valeria persuaded him to sit down in an armchair and helped him to soup and a glass of brandy.

He thanked her with a sigh.

"Miss Montford," he began. "Lord Waterford has suffered concussion. I have shaved the area around the wound and stitched it up. He was lucky not to have had his skull cracked open. As it is, there is a minor fracture."

"Minor?" Valeria's heart lifted a little. "Then he will recover?"

"I cannot say, Miss Montford. An injury such as this one could mean the patient remaining in a coma for some considerable time. He may regain consciousness or – "

His shoulders lifted in a small shrug.

Valeria went icy cold.

"What can be done for him?" she whispered.

"Keep him warm, that is extremely important. Try to feed him a little broth from time to time. Talk to him.

"We never know how much unconscious patients can hear and I have known of cases where family – and

125

friends," he added with a compassionate look at Valeria, "continually talk to their loved ones and they might very well have played a part in their recovery."

"I will do everything I can and I am sure that Lady Stratfield will do all in her power to help too."

"You seem a sensible young lady, Miss Montford, and Lord Waterford appears fortunate in his staff. I will arrange for nurses, but I do repeat that it is familiar voices around him that may prove the best cure.

"It is essential that his Lordship is watched over at all times. I have left his valet sitting by his bed. The butler has assured me that all the staff are willing to take on this duty. He appears to have earned considerable loyalty."

He finished his soup noisily, downed the glass of brandy and then stood up, apparently refreshed.

"I shall be back in the morning – "

The moment the doctor had left, Valeria went back upstairs to Lord Waterford's bedroom.

She gave a soft knock on the door.

The valet opened it.

"How is his Lordship, George?"

"Struggling, Miss Montford, definitely struggling."

Valeria gently pushed open the door and stepped into the room.

"I have come to sit with his Lordship. The doctor says it will help for friends and relations to talk to him."

The valet looked rather doubtful and Valeria sat on the chair beside the bed.

"I will be here if anything should be needed, Miss Montford," murmured George.

Nothing seemed to have changed in the condition of Lord Waterford.

Valeria's heart contracted as she saw how bloodless his face seemed to be and heard once again the laboured manner of his breathing.

Gently she took his hand in hers. It was cold and she started to rub it gently, looking at him closely to see if there was any indication that he felt her touch.

There was nothing.

Speaking calmly, she began,

"Lord Waterford, it is Valeria. I saw you attacked. I am so sorry for your injury, but Doctor Marshall says that it is minor and that you will soon be well. I have come to tell you all about the textiles I selected yesterday."

As she said this, Valeria remembered her encounter with Sir Peter and she took a quick breath.

Then she forced the memory away.

She never wished to see Sir Peter again.

She knew now that the only man who could ever mean anything to her was the one lying here on the bed in front of her.

As she talked, she looked at the contours of the face she now knew so well.

She allowed her eyes to gaze, almost greedily, on his beautifully chiselled cheekbones, the well-shaped nose, the fine mouth, now slightly open.

The eyes, that could crinkle so with laughter, that could be so kind and so searching, were closed and it was as though a door had been closed on Lord Waterford, the man Valeria so wanted to be able to call by his given name.

'Charles' was such a splendid name.

Had she now lost *all* chance, all possibility of him looking at her again with the love that had been in his eyes at the beginning? Then she had scorned him, then she had fallen for the easy flashy charms of Sir Peter Cousins.

Looking back at her past with the two men, Valeria mourned her stupidity.

Lord Waterford had never humiliated her, she had humiliated herself.

She had desired surface glitter, easy compliments, the sort of smart chat that meant nothing.

Now she felt older and wiser. Now she knew that true love was like a plant with roots deep in the earth that could not easily be damaged by wind or flood.

Valeria paused in her account of matching braids and fringes for The Castle.

More than anything in the world she wanted to tell Lord Waterford, *Charles*, that she loved him more than life itself.

But the valet sitting at the back of the room stopped her. So instead she concentrated on telling him everything she had planned for The Castle. It would not matter that most of it he already knew.

The thing was to keep talking.

For Valeria it was as if her voice was providing a thread that could drag the man she loved back from some dark unknown fate.

At some point the valet opened the curtains and the light gradually strengthened until the sun rose and another lovely day dawned.

For her, however, the day could never be blessed with any sunshine until the man lying senseless on the bed managed to open his eyes and smile at her.

Someone brought her coffee, placed it on a small table by her side and begged her to drink it.

Her voice was hoarse with the hours of talking and she kept her hold of Lord Waterford's hand, but managed to savour the coffee gratefully at the same time, continuing talking between sips.

Later Doctor Marshall arrived back, bringing with him a sensible-looking nurse.

He looked startled to see Valeria by the bed, Lord Waterford's hand firmly in her grasp and still dressed in the same simple gown she was wearing last night.

Reluctantly she released his hand and rose.

The valet came forward and looked at his Master.

"He seems better. His breathing is easier."

It was true, Valeria realised. It still was not normal, but the awful snoring aspect had softened.

"I will let you examine your patient, doctor," said Valeria and left the room.

Outside she leaned against the door for a moment.

Exhaustion flooded over her and she had to sit on one of the chairs in the corridor.

"Valeria, my dear, have you been here all night?" Susan laid a hand on her shoulder. "How is Charles?"

Valeria closed her eyes for a moment.

"Still unconscious. The doctor's with him. He has brought a nurse."

"That's splendid. I am sure that Charles will soon be back with us. Come with me, let us go and have some breakfast, you look quite done in."

Gently she helped Valeria to her feet and took her downstairs to the morning room.

Halfway through breakfast, the butler appeared.

"My Lady, may I have a few words, please?"

"Of course, Hawkins. What is it? Oh, don't worry about Miss Montford, you can speak in front of her."

"It is just that – it is a question of contacting the police, my Lady."

"The police!" Susan sounded horrified.

"Lord Waterford has been attacked, my Lady."

Susan sat still, drumming her fingers on the table.

"Do we know why my brother was in the Park?"

"No, my Lady."

"Thank you, Hawkins. We'll speak about it again later. But for now, *no* police."

"No, my Lady."

Hawkins glided from the room.

Susan looked at Valeria.

"And how was it that *you* were there too, ready to scream for help?"

Valeria blushed deep crimson and could not think of anying sensible to say.

Susan's eyes narrowed suspiciously.

"Last night an old friend of mine mentioned seeing you in the company of a certain Sir Peter Cousins in an unlikely area on the edge of City. I said he must have been mistaken. But was he?"

Again, Valeria could think of nothing to say.

"Were you slipping out for a rendezvous with that devil in Green Park? God knows, enough women imagine that he is attractive."

She looked flustered.

"I suppose I had better confess that I was once one of them. But the man is a cad. I would not have dreamed you could be involved with him, but your silence has to be read as guilt."

"*No!* Sir Peter means nothing to me."

"And so you were not meeting him in the Park last night?"

"Of course not.

"But you were there – and so was my brother."

Valeria could not bring herself to say she believed that it was Lord Waterford who had the assignation.

Susan put her hand to her forehead.

"This is all too much for me. I cannot be expected to make sense of a situation which is impossible to fathom. It will have to wait until Charles regains consciousness.

"But," her voice sharpened. "Till then, we shall not have the police interfering around here. Charles must have been attacked by a cowardly thief and there would be no witnesses and the police would be unlikely to find who it was, so it would be useless to involve them."

Then the doctor was shown into the room.

Susan immediately rose and went to him.

"How is my poor brother, doctor?"

"Your Ladyship, Miss Montford, I am pleased to report that Lord Waterford does seem a little better today. He is still unconscious, however, and I would suggest that talking to him as I understand that Miss Montford has been doing, can do nothing but good."

After assuring them that he would return later that day Doctor Marshall took his leave.

Susan looked at Valeria.

"You have been talking to Charles?"

"Only of the most ordinary of matters such as the restoration work at The Castle. The doctor said it could be very beneficial for a familiar voice to talk to him, although whether he is capable of hearing is a question that cannot be answered."

"Then, I suppose – " muttered Susan indecisively, "it is my duty to go and sit with him."

Valeria followed her upstairs. The little breakfast she had eaten had given her renewed energy.

Susan approached the bed and looked down at her unconscious brother. The nurse sitting by the bed rose on her entrance and dipped a curtsy.

"There is no change, my Lady."

Valeria saw Susan grip her hands together.

"Oh, oh, Charles!" she moaned.

She collapsed onto the chair, then placed her head in her hands and burst into a storm of weeping.

Valeria placed an arm around her.

"Come along, Susan, this will not do him any good, you must be strong, come with me and we will find your maid and a soothing draught."

Later Valeria left Susan lying on her bed, returned to Lord Waterford's bedroom and once again sat with him, holding his hand and talking to him.

This time she related the story of her stay in France, their meeting out on the hillside and the rescue of the little girl in the Château moat.

"You were so brave," she reminisced, with a catch in her voice. "Without you I think both Marie and I would have drowned."

The nurse moved slightly and Valeria realised that she too, if not the unconscious man, had been enthralled by the story she had heard.

Valeria's voice was by now no more than a croak and not even a cup of tea could rescue it.

Hawkins came to her side.

"Miss Montford, you must have a rest. It will be of

no use to his Lordship if you collapse. After a rest you can return and take up your watch again."

His craggy face was kind and Valeria realised that he understood just how concerned she was for his Master.

She realised that he was right. She was so tired she could hardly stand.

"Thank you, Hawkins. You are most thoughtful."

"I will talk to his Lordship for a while. He knows my voice well."

Wearily she dragged herself to her room. Her maid helped her out of her dress and into bed.

"Please wake me up in an hour," asked Valeria as she sank into sleep.

*

It was, however, much, much later when she finally awoke. Donning a fresh gown, she went quickly to Lord Waterford's bedroom.

Little had changed in his condition and he seemed no nearer consciousness.

The butler had given way to the valet, who was in the middle of a long description of a new fashion. When he saw Valeria, he jumped up so she could take his place.

Once again Valeria took hold of Lord Waterford's hand and talked to him of everything they had done since coming to London for the Queen's Jubilee.

As she talked him through all the Celebration balls, she suddenly thought of Lady Mere, of the assignations she was convinced were the reason for his nightly visits to the Park.

The longer she remained at Lord Waterford's side, talking to him, the more she thought about Lady Mere.

Had she been frightened off by the attack on Lord Waterford? Was she awaiting news of him?

Later that evening, Hawkins appeared and said he would relieve her for a while.

"Hawkins, has anybody called at the house today enquiring after Lord Waterford?"

Hawkins looked surprised.

"Why, no, miss. No one."

How odd. But perhaps, decided Valeria's exhausted mind, Lady Mere did not want to betray her involvement with Lord Waterford. Perhaps, even now, she was waiting in Green Park to see if he would come to her.

Valeria knew how consumed with worry she would be in her place, so she decided she must go into Green Park and see if a woman was waiting there.

She refused to listen to a small voice at the back of her mind that said maybe she, herself, might be attacked.

She went into the drawing room and opened one of the French windows. It was another warm night. No need for any sort of wrap.

Noiselessly she slipped out of the house. Then she was in Green Park itself, surrounded by the tall trees, the green grass stretching ahead of her.

Lying on the ground like the previous night were any number of sleeping figures.

She could not see anyone standing near the house, male or female, but the amount of greenery around the end of the garden made it difficult to see.

Valeria stepped a little way into the Park.

Almost immediately two shrouded figures began to move threateningly towards her.

CHAPTER TEN

Valeria was too terrified to scream.

She wanted to turn and run back to the house, but her tired body refused to obey.

The two figures ambled up to her.

They were tramps, their clothes ragged and dirty with broken boots tied onto their feet with string, but they no longer seemed quite so threatening.

"'Ow's the gent, then," asked the first one.

Valeria remained frozen to the spot.

"It was you 'ere last night, wasn't it, missus?"

Valeria pulled herself together and thought that she knew what this was all about.

"It was *you* who fought Lord Waterford's attacker, wasn't it?"

The two men shuffled in an embarrassed manner.

"'E's a good sort, you see," said the first. "Wanted to give Alf and me a chance for a new life."

"Our mate, Percy, 'e'd already taken 'im up on it and Bob 'ere thought 'e'd 'ave a go," the second explained.

"A new life?" Valeria exclaimed, bewildered.

"'Ere, let's go nearer the 'ouse. Don't want no one gangin' up on you, miss."

They melted into the shade of a large shrub by the garden gate. Valeria, suspicious but feeling that, so close to the house, there was little to fear, moved nearer to them.

"Now," she began, "maybe you can tell me exactly what this is all about. "

Gradually, as she questioned the two of them, it all became clear.

Lord Waterford had offered to provide these down-and-outs with jobs on his country estate. He had told them he had a place where they could live, jobs for them, as long as they did not mind hard work.

"We'd said we'd give it a go," added Bob.

Now that her eyes were accustomed to the dark, she could make out a lined face with beetle eyebrows.

"Sleepin' in the Park's alright when the weather's like this, but in winter and rain and snow it ain't no joke."

"At first we thought it were a scam of some sort," Alf came in – taller than Bob, his face even more lined.

"Didn't seem to be any reason why a bang-up cove like 'im would take any notice of, well, chaps like us, so us says if he returned another night and made the same offer, then we'd prob'ly take it."

"So Lord Waterford hasn't been meeting a woman in the Park?" Valeria enquired hopefully.

"Lor' luv a duck no! Is that what folks thought?"

"Only *me*," she assured them, "I don't think anyone else was aware that he was meeting anyone in the Park."

"'Ow is he? 'Ell of a whack that blighter give 'im."

"He's been unconscious ever since," said Valeria, tears coming to her eyes as a vision of Lord Waterford's inert body flashed before her eyes.

"You were very good to go for that man, whoever he was. You didn't see him properly, I suppose?"

Bob shook his head gloomily.

"'E 'ad an 'ood on. And he 'opped it pretty damn quick, pardon my language, miss, but if I comes across 'im any time during the next week or so, I'll know 'im by the bloody great scars my nails made on 'is face, I got right under that Balaclava!"

"An' I clopped 'im 'ard one on the ear," added Alf. "Any chance of the toff still givin' us a chance, eh?"

Valeria thought quickly.

Lord Waterford had suffered a nasty blow on the head that might yet prove fatal.

However, without these two men, he could well be dead. They deserved some reward.

The fact that Lord Waterford appeared to be set on a mission of saving the poor and helpless shone a new light on the man Valeria loved.

He wanted Bob and Alf to have a second chance at life. Each of them looked no more than middle-aged.

"Can you remain here for a little?" she asked. "I'm going to see if something can be done. At the very least you are due a reward for what you did."

Bob and Alf assured her they would not move from where they stood.

Inside the house, Valeria went back upstairs to Lord Waterford's bedroom.

Hawkins was sitting beside the bed, recalling all the arrangements that had been made for the Waterford Ball.

Valeria asked if he would spare her a few moments outside.

Then she put the situation to him.

"You never went by yourself into Green Park at this hour?" Hawkins was obviously horrified. "Miss Montford, what would his Lordship say?"

Then they were both silent for a little until Hawkins cleared his throat.

"Miss Montford, we are all very conscious of your devotion in trying to awaken his Lordship. He is a man we all value."

He paused for a moment and then continued,

"I believe his Lordship would want these men sent to The Castle. There are already quite a number of these unhappy victims of fortune there. I will provide the two you have talked to with a note to the Agent and he will do the necessary. Perhaps you will take me to them."

This was done.

Alf and Bob both followed Hawkins happily into the house and Valeria felt relief.

It seemed that Lord Waterford did not have a secret love after all.

Now the truth had been revealed, Valeria realised that meeting females in secret at dead of night was not the sort of activity he would undertake and it was only her fear that she had lost his love that had made her think so.

Silently she apologised to Lord Waterford and Lady Mere for her wayward thoughts.

She returned to his bedside, took hold of his hand once again and wondered what she could tell him now.

After a little thought, she embarked on an account of her parents and their love for each other.

Deep into the night she talked, once again her voice becoming hoarse.

In the early hours the nurse came and stood behind her. She placed a hand on Valeria's shoulder and pressed lightly.

"His Lordship's coming round. See his breathing is normal and look – his eyelids are fluttering."

Valeria held her breath as his eyes opened.

He gave her a sweet smile and whispered,

"What happened?"

"Someone hit you," Valeria told him, clutching his hand tightly. "You will be all right now."

"Good," came another faint whisper.

Then Lord Waterford closed his eyes again.

"He's asleep," whispered the nurse.

Tears began to run down Valeria's face.

She released his hand, smoothing it lovingly with hers before standing up and moving away from the bed.

She put her face in her hands and sobbed silently.

The nurse put an arm around her shoulders.

"There, there, miss. It's been such a dreadful time for you and you have done wonderfully well. His Lordship should be very proud of you."

Valeria shook her head.

"I mean nothing to him," she whispered, sobbing as quietly as she could manage. "But I am very happy he has come round."

"There is some way to go yet," the nurse warned, "but I think he will make it now. However, you had better be prepared for difficulties and problems."

*

The following day Valeria began to realise what the nurse had meant.

The recovering Lord Waterford became dictatorial and dismissive. He was like an autocratic child.

When Valeria came in to see him the next morning, he asked who she was –

Doctor Marshall, on one of his regular visits, took Valeria from the room.

"It is quite common with patients recovering from concussion," he counselled. "Give him a few days and he will recover his memory and become once again the man you know. He may, however, never recall being attacked."

This was not much consolation to Valeria.

Having agonised so deeply over him and shared so many stories with him and as she talked to him for so long, it was difficult to accept that she appeared to mean nothing to him now.

He cannot, she thought, have heard even one of the thousands and thousands of words she had spoken to him.

The mistress she had imagined might not exist, but it appeared that for Lord Waterford, she, Valeria Montford, did not exist either.

She had been wiped from his consciousness.

She laid no confidence in the doctor's assertion that he would soon return to his normal self.

After all, what was his normal self?

Was it the man who loved and wanted her for his wife? Or the kindly somewhat distant man he had become after throwing Sir Peter out of The Castle, the man who did not seem at all interested in her as a woman?

Soon Valeria became even more upset.

Now her brother had regained consciousness, Susan was only too eager to spend time with him and seemed to insinuate that Valeria had no place at his side.

The suspicious attitude she had adopted over what Valeria had been doing in the Park remained.

She still seemed, despite Valeria's many denials, to believe she had planned an assignation with Sir Peter.

*

At breakfast two days later, Valeria received a note from her father saying that he had not had the pleasure of her company for far too long. He would call for her later that morning and take her for a ride in his open carriage.

Valeria told Susan of this invitation.

"But I think I should refuse. You could need me to attend on Lord Waterford?"

"No, I don't think so. I am more than capable of handling my brother. Indeed, I think the strain of coping with someone outside the family circle would be too much for him in his present delicate state."

Valeria stared at her aghast.

"I understand," she replied stiffly. "I will talk to my father about returning to my home."

"I think that will be for the best," sniffed Susan.

*

Valeria greeted her beloved Papa with delight.

It was great to be enfolded in his arms again and then carefully helped into his curricle.

"I thought, Valeria, that we would call at our home for a few minutes and then go for a trip in Richmond Park. It will be looking quite beautiful at this time of the year."

"Oh, Papa, that sounds wonderful."

Stepping inside their delightful home, Valeria felt a deep deep sadness.

Since the evening spent with Lord Waterford here, everything seemed to have gone wrong. She had hoped to create a similarly beautiful atmosphere at The Castle.

And for some time things had appeared to go well.

If only Sir Peter had not arrived in her life to upset her emotions with his extraordinary personality.

For a moment she wondered how she would react if she met him again.

Would he somehow, insidiously, pierce through her

intense dislike of him and make her yearn for his embrace? Even to want to marry him?

The very thought made her shudder and *yet* –

Then she dismissed the man from her mind.

She knew without any doubt at all that it was Lord Waterford she loved. If only, she thought wistfully, he still loved her!

There was a letter waiting for Valeria from Juliette. She hastily read it while her father collected their picnic.

She gasped just as he came to tell her all was ready.

"What is in that letter?" he asked.

"Juliette tells me that Lord Waterford has rescued a French family we met when I was there. They were in dire poverty and now he has arranged that the father has been given work on the estate of his French friend and they have a proper cottage to live in. And Lord Waterford is paying for the boy to go to school!"

She looked at her father, her face glowing.

"He is such a wonderful man, Papa."

Once they were back in the carriage, they set off.

"Are you at last going to accept Lord Waterford, this '*wonderful man*', my darling?"

"Oh, Papa, I don't think he wants to marry me any longer," Valeria said with a long sigh of hopelessness.

As they bowled along towards Richmond Park, she told the story to her father.

She did not, however, mention Sir Peter by name. It was really as though, if she did not identify him, he did not really exist.

"Well, sweetheart," he said in a rallying voice when she had finished, "I do not think you need despair. When Lord Waterford has properly recovered, I am sure he will want to resume your friendship and then he will fall in love with you all over again. After all is said and done, you have been responsible for saving his life."

"Not really. It was Alf and Bob who rescued him from that criminal who wanted to rob him."

"It was *you* who warned him and then looked after him so lovingly."

"But he does not even know I was there. He was unconscious. Oh, Papa, apart from my happiness, what will happen to you if I don't marry a rich man? I believe that now I can build a good career for myself as an interior designer, but what about you?"

For a moment he concentrated on driving through the gates into Richmond Park and he then laid a comforting hand on Valeria's knee.

"Don't you worry about me, darling. I will sell the house and probably go and live abroad where it is so much cheaper and my expertise with horses will, I feel very sure, be much in demand."

"You don't think of marrying again?" she enquired, remembering the way he had looked at Lady Braithwaite.

"I thought at one time that I might, but I had such happiness with your dear Mama, I find I cannot replace her in my heart. No, I will be fine, it is *you* I worry about."

Valeria was deeply touched at his care for her and would have said much more but a rider came up and trotted alongside them.

"*Well met again indeed*," crowed Sir Peter Cousins, on her father's side of the carriage.

He tipped his whip to his hat and flashed Valeria his devastating smile.

"I have been waiting for just such an opportunity."

Sir Christopher gave a sudden exclamation.

"*You!*" he cried.

Valeria gazed at Sir Peter in horror.

A short while ago she had wondered if a meeting with him would arouse any feelings of desire in her breast.

Now she recognised that the only emotion she felt was disgust.

But before she could tell him to leave her alone, her Papa lashed out at Sir Peter with his whip.

"How dare you, sir! First you ruin me and now you have the temerity to address my daughter."

Sir Peter wrenched the whip out of his hand.

"What a useless excuse for a man you are. If you had any sense, you would have known the scheme I offered you for the fake it was. I took your money and now I shall take your daughter!"

With a coarse laugh, he manoeuvred his horse right beside the carriage. Then he reached across and grabbed Sir Christopher and then with incredible power pulled him out of the carriage and thrust him onto the ground.

Valeria screamed and tried to take hold of the reins as the horses, now driverless, careered forward.

Her Papa was left lying on the road behind them.

Sir Peter swung himself off his horse and into the curricle. He yanked the reins away from Valeria and urged the horses to even greater speed.

Valeria beat at him with her fists, but she knew it was useless – he was now in the driving seat.

Twisting around, she saw her father sitting on the grass, his head in his hands. At least he did not seem badly injured.

Sir Peter flicked the reins.

"Get on with it," he roared at the horses.

A manic laugh came from him.

"I have you, my darling," he shouted at Valeria. "You will be mine! I have always sworn it and now there is nothing to stop me. I have it all planned."

Valeria was terrified.

The man was out of control. She could not believe that she had ever felt attracted by him. And to now know that he was the devil who had ruined her father was doubly shocking.

Suddenly she noticed deep scratches running down from forehead to chin on the left-hand side of his face.

In a moment's blinding realisation, she cried out,

"It was *you* who attacked Lord Waterford in Green Park!"

"That damned man," screamed Sir Peter, standing in the carriage, now rocking dangerously and lashing at the horses with the reins.

"He was stealing you from me, I knew it."

He sat down again, trying to control the direction of the horses, now galloping far too fast.

"Waiting is a game I know. I had waited for you to emerge from Waterford House. I waited for that damned Peer to come into the Park. I just knew that he would. If it hadn't been for those idiotic tramps, I would have rid the world of him entirely. I waited for him to die!

"Then I heard from your father's lady friend that he was taking you for a spin in Richmond Park today. So I waited again – *and then you appeared!*"

Sir Peter put an arm around her shoulders, drawing her close.

Valeria shuddered.

He bent to kiss her.

Disgust rose in her throat. Desperately she pushed against his chest with all her strength, just as the path they were driving so rapidly along came to a bend.

Coming in the other direction was another carriage.

Sir Peter cursed loudly and tried to regain control of the curricle whilst it veered crazily as the horses missed the turn.

The wheels left the road and struck a large rock.

Valeria screamed and grabbed at the curricle's side as it overturned.

Both of them were thrown out.

Valeria landed on top of Sir Peter and then ended up on the grass, all breath knocked out of her.

The horses continued for a little, pulling the broken curricle behind them.

Sir Peter's left foot was caught in the reins and he was dragged along the ground. Then the broken spokes of one of the wheels were forced into his unconscious body.

Lost in horror, Valeria slipped into darkness.

*

She soon came to.

The air was filled with snorting horses and excited chatter.

Valeria's head was in her father's lap.

A cruel graze on his forehead dripped blood down one side of his face, but otherwise he seemed unharmed.

"My darling Valeria," he cautioned. "Don't move. Someone has gone for a stretcher."

Valeria found it impossible to obey him. Gingerly as she remembered lying on the ground after falling from her horse in France, she moved first her arms and then her legs. Much to her relief, once again everything seemed to be in working order.

"Are you all right, Papa?" she breathed, feeling safe with his beloved arms around her.

"By the Grace of God, I seem to be. Fortunately, we were driving quite slowly when that fiend pushed me out. I was able to pick myself up and follow after you. I reached the scene of the disaster not long after it occurred."

"Sir Peter?" she asked apprehensively, the memory of the peril she had been in filled her even now with terror.

"*Dead*. I can only feel relief that such a villain has left this life – and well deserved too."

She closed her eyes again, this time in thankfulness.

That anyone should meet such a dreadful end was a tragedy in itself, but he would no longer be able to defraud innocent people such as her father and prey on vulnerable girls such as herself.

She retained little memory of the next few hours.

Later she learned that willing hands had placed her into a most comfortable carriage and brought her back to her Richmond home.

There she was put to bed and her old family doctor was sent for. He pronounced her badly bruised and with a sprained ankle.

Otherwise she had experienced a miraculous escape and both her body and her mind now needed complete rest.

Visitors would not be allowed and she should have a nourishing but light diet and he would prescribe a tonic.

Her Papa arranged for her maid to pack everything of hers still at Waterford House and bring all her luggage back to Richmond.

As soon as Mary appeared, she enquired anxiously about Lord Waterford.

Mary grinned.

"Much better, Miss Montford. George says he's a right handful, which be a good sign."

Valeria lay back in her bed with thankfulness.

"Her Ladyship is in a right state about me bringing everything back here. She is to write to you, her maid told me."

The letter arrived the next day.

Susan feared that Valeria had misunderstood some words of hers.

She would not have had her dear friend leave the house so suddenly – maybe later when Lord Waterford was recovered, they would be able to renew their friendship.

Valeria, her body so battered and bruised, her ankle aching and her spirits lower than they had ever been since the death of her Mama, cast the letter onto the floor.

Her Papa, entering her bedroom, picked it up.

"A word of cheer from a friend, I would hope, my darling?"

Valeria turned away, tears pricking at her eyes.

"I thought she was a friend – but now I doubt it."

Soon she was recovered enough to receive visitors, who did their best to revive her spirits.

Among the first callers were Sir Patrick and Lady Waverley, who had been driving in the carriage coming in the opposite direction.

They had been mortified at having caused such a nasty accident. To them and to them alone, the full details behind the incident were explained.

The rest of the world was allowed to think that Sir Christopher had permitted Sir Peter to take the reins of his pair for a drive prior to making an offer for them and that Valeria had merely been an innocent passenger.

It had been a wonderful release to be able to tell the truth and the Waverleys had sworn to keep the story secret.

*

Later Valeria's spirits were not helped by a friend reading out to her an item from a newspaper one day that announced Lord Waterford, recovered from a mysterious illness, had retired to The Castle, his country home.

"I expect," remarked her friend, "that you will soon be receiving an invitation to visit him again."

She tried to dampen any expectations, but her heart plummeted at the news.

She had so hoped that Lord Waterford would, at the least, have sent her a note wishing her a rapid recovery, as there had been a report in another edition of the newspaper of her accident in Richmond Park.

Suddenly Valeria realised with horrid finality that the Waterfords, seeing Sir Peter's name in the report would have assumed that she was his willing companion. Susan already believed she was enamoured of him.

Despairingly she wondered if she should write to Lord Waterford and tell him the truth.

Then she decided he would not believe her.

However, several days later, her Papa, opening the mail at breakfast, read a letter and glanced across at Valeria with a broad smile.

"Cheer up, my darling, I have splendid news. Lord Waterford has invited us both to The Castle for a stay."

Valeria was thunderstruck.

"No! It cannot be! What reason does he give?"

"Aha, so you do believe me. He says that you will want to see how splendid The Castle looks these days and he wants to thank you for all your work and inspiration."

Her heart, which had risen briefly, dropped again.

This was the polite gesture of a gentleman.

Nothing suggested the eager lover.

"Shall we accept?" her Papa asked gently.

Despite her decision to put Lord Waterford and her love for him behind her, Valeria could not help saying,

"Yes, Papa, *we should go*."

*

The first sight of The Castle almost reduced Valeria to tears. This was where she had fallen so deeply in love.

This was place she had invested so much time in, so much emotion and so much commitment.

"I say," her Papa commented. "What a place!"

"The restoration work has proceeded apace," said Lord Waterford's Steward.

He had met them at the station explaining that Lord Waterford was still not quite recovered from his accident and awaited them at The Castle.

As they drew nearer, Valeria gasped.

The Steward smiled.

"It looks wonderful, does it not, the moat?"

When she had left, the moat had had the appearance of a broad ditch filled with rubbish. Now it had all been cleared and grass was growing within its graceful lines.

Waiting beside The Castle's heavy door was Lord Waterford. He walked forward to open the carriage door, pre-empting the groom.

Valeria hungrily studied him closely as he helped her down.

His hair was cut short to match the regrowth around his scar. His face was thinner and looked careworn. Was it her imagination or did it light up at the sight of her?

No, she told herself, he was just smiling politely.

In The Castle Susan kissed Valeria and appeared as friendly as she had ever been.

The reception rooms had been restored exactly as Valeria had designed. They looked magnificent and her Papa said so enthusiastically.

Valeria expressed her amazement at the speed with which the work had been carried out.

Lord Waterford smiled.

"I offered a large bonus to the building firm."

Dinner was taken early.

Valeria was so grateful that her Papa was one of the party. Susan was unaccustomedly quiet but Lord Waterford was courteous and exchanged a flow of anecdotes with Sir Christopher about horses and breeding.

He hardly looked at Valeria, however, and she grew more and more silent as the dinner progressed.

At the end of dinner, Susan announced that she and Valeria would not be leaving the gentlemen to their port.

"I wish to show Sir Christopher the stables before the light disappears," she explained with a charming smile. "Will you come with me, sir, my brother feels it would be too much for him just yet?"

She held out her hand and he appeared happy to go with her.

Lord Waterford rose.

"I would be very grateful if you would accompany me onto The Castle ramparts," he invited Valeria. "There is something I would like to show you."

More than willing but mystified as to what it could be, she followed him up the stone spiral staircase, worrying that the climb would take too much out of him.

He seemed not at all out of breath when they next emerged onto the battlement walk.

He smiled at Valeria and took her over to where they could look down into the moat.

"I want you to imagine how it will look next year, when deer will be grazing there," he commented, watching her closely.

Valeria drew a quick breath.

"Why," she murmured, "I was going to suggest just that same idea to you."

It was why she had walked all the way round the castle the time that Sir Peter had drawn her into the woods. She flushed as she remembered the incident and her fatal response.

Lord Waterford looked surprised.

"But you *did* suggest it," he countered. "As soon as I returned here, I remembered you telling me your idea and it sounded so good, I immediately set the work of clearing the moat in progress."

Valeria opened her mouth to say that she had been saving up this idea to suggest it to him after the Jubilee Celebrations, when she had hoped she would be invited to return to The Castle.

Then she realised what must have happened.

"*You did hear me!*" she exclaimed.

"Of course, I heard everything you have ever said to me," replied Lord Waterford, looking perplexed.

"No, I mean when you were unconscious. Doctor Marshall urged me to talk to you. I spoke of many things about the restoration. Most of them we had discussed, but this was something I had not mentioned before."

Lord Waterford took her hand.

"I have not thanked you yet for all your care of me whilst I was lying in a coma. George told me exactly how much time you spent at my side. He is a big fan of yours."

Valeria blushed.

"You have very loyal servants, my Lord."

Lord Waterford looked down.

"Tell me," he said without raising his gaze. "What were you doing in Green Park that night? Susan believed you expected to meet Sir Peter, although now she is less certain and is apologetic about the way she spoke to you."

Then he raised his eyes and Valeria felt a flood of emotion rush through her, as though some dam had broken.

"My Lord, I had *no* wish to meet Sir Peter. I admit I once admired his – his energy."

It was the only word she could think of to explain the effect the dreadful man had had on her.

Lord Waterford closed his eyes briefly.

"But then I understood what a very unpleasant and dastardly character he was."

He looked intently at her.

"So I realised after my old friends, the Waverleys, visited here the other day. When they had found out how closely involved you and I were, they explained all that had happened in Richmond Park and how you were injured."

He picked up her hand gently.

"I was mortified not to have been told the facts and not to have been able to express my wishes for your speedy recovery. And after all you did for me – "

His voice faltered and stopped.

Valeria was unable to say anything.

She scanned his face, trying in the dying light to interpret his expression.

Electricity seemed to be travelling from his hand into hers, spreading throughout her body and making her limbs tremble.

"So why were you in the Park that night?" Lord Waterford repeated, his gaze never leaving her face.

Once again Valeria blushed deeply.

"I was afraid you were meeting someone else."

He looked startled.

"Someone else?"

"You had seemed very attracted to, well, I will not mention the name – but she was at a number of the parties we – attended – "

Valeria stammered to a halt.

He laughed in amazement.

"I can only imagine that you saw me talking and dancing with Frances Mere. She is extremely pretty, but my only interest in her is as a childhood friend."

Valeria realised that, once again, she had jumped to a wrong conclusion over Lord Waterford.

He raised her hands and gently kissed her fingers.

"If you were that interested in where my affections lay, dare I now hope that your feelings towards me have changed since I first admitted my love for you?

"I am very different now, Valeria. Then I was a romantic fool, but you have shown me what true love is."

Valeria looked at him with unaccustomed shyness, her heart beating so fast she thought it might explode.

"Do you mean that – you still love me?"

"Of course. How could you ever doubt that?"

"You – you seemed so removed from me when we arrived in London."

"I was so in love with you that I could hardly trust myself to be near you without taking you in my arms – like this."

Valeria sank into Lord Waterford's embrace with a sweet familiarity that astonished her.

It seemed so natural and yet so wonderful.

As his arms clasped her, his lips met hers and the sweetness increased until she believed she had been carried up to Heaven.

Nothing she had felt when being kissed by Sir Peter compared with this exquisite sensation.

"Oh!" she exclaimed when at last he raised his head from hers and gazed into her eyes with such adoration she could hardly believe what she saw.

"Oh – kiss me again."

He laughed, drew her even closer to his breast and kissed her even more passionately.

"I never want to stop," he murmured at last, raising his head. "I have found Paradise."

"Yes, my dearest Charles. That is just what I feel. Your kisses are flying me to the moon and beyond."

"And you will not mind if I continue to rescue poor souls and put them in that house you once asked me what I planned to do with, when I was stupid enough to be afraid you would think me silly if I told you of my intentions?"

Valeria laughed softly.

"I am looking forward to meeting with Alf and Bob again and all the others you have found."

"When I was told you had organised with Hawkins for them to come down here, I was sure I could risk asking you again to be my wife –

"I love and adore you, Valeria, and will throughout Eternity and I know you will love me too for just as long."

Valeria smiled and laid her head on his chest.

As his arms closed gently around her again, she just knew that, despite everything, she had found the happiness she had always sought here at The Castle with the man she loved and would never leave.